KISS OF DEATH

SUPERNATURAL SECURITY FORCE, BOOK 1

HEATHER HILDENBRAND

Kiss of Death

Supernatural Security Force, Book 1

By Heather Hildenbrand

ISBN 9781708432126

DEDICATION

To the woman who asked if I think I need curse words in
my books just so people will buy them.
The answer is no. But it's a lot more fun.

ONE

The punk behind me was right on my ass. Adrenaline pumped through me until my magic hummed at the same vibration as the engine's purr. Eyes locked on the pavement ahead, I pressed my foot harder on the gas and let the speed take over. Stress and worry fell away. Problems didn't matter. For this forty seconds of asphalt, it was just me and the expert piece of machinery I now controlled.

"Eat our dust, bitchnuggets!"

Okay, me and Gran.

"Gran, you can't call people bitchnuggets," I said.

"Why the hell not?"

"I don't know. Maybe because no one else's grandma makes up weird curse words."

"No one else's grandma is a fucking beetle either."

She had a point.

Last year, my grandpa Cal had passed away in his

sleep. The next morning, overcome by grief, two things had happened to Gran. First, she accidentally shapeshifted into a June bug and lost the ability to shift back. And two, after realizing she was stuck in the body of an insect, she'd developed a potty mouth worse than a drunken sailor at Mardi Gras.

My mother was mortified by Gran's new vocabulary, but I mostly just rolled with it. I'd be pissed too if I couldn't change back to a form that included opposable thumbs. Or any creature whose number one predator wasn't a mole or prairie dog.

"Shitmonkeys, he's gainin' on ya," Gran said.

"I see it." My gaze slid to the rearview and then back to the road.

"Well?" Gran said. "Kick his ass already."

"I'm working on it, Gran. Stop distracting me."

A buzzing along my outer ear was my only answer.

"Hey, I'm trying to drive." I swatted her away.

She huffed and landed on the dashboard again.

Just ahead, the road wound sharply left. It was a turn I'd made a thousand times without so much as a tire over the edge of the pavement. Anticipation built in my stomach, and I held my breath as I whipped the wheel around with one hand. With the other, I gripped the shifter. *Tight and loose.* It was the mantra Juice had taught me that I now repeated to myself over and over as the street lamps fell away, washing the view ahead in darkness.

The only light came from my headlights, and that wasn't much help at this speed.

Eighty-five.

Ninety.

Ninety-five.

My personal best on this stretch was 101.

The highest speed on record was 112, but that guy hadn't made the S-turn. I wasn't interested in beating his record if it meant hydroplaning off the edge of the bulkhead and into the river churning below.

My tires hugged the corner as I went into the first of the double turn.

"Yeehaw," Gran called.

My vision sharpened, the headlights not quite keeping up with the front end as I whipped expertly around the switchback curve.

The cool night air seeped in around me, but my insides were hot. Intent on the speed, the precision, and the Jetta coming up on my right.

"Gem, this little pissant is makin' a move," Gran said in warning.

"I see it."

Asshole thought he could take me on the inside.

I snorted, my eyes darting to the mirror that showed his front bumper inching closer.

Dumbass was still giving it gas.

He'd regret that in about eight seconds.

The second half of the switchback sent my tires screaming. I smiled to myself, knowing full well I'd just kicked up a solid cloud of smoke for my opponent. It also meant I'd need a new set of tires after tonight. Juice was going to go off, but it was worth it.

A second later, my fae hearing proved me right. The roar of the Jetta's engine dialed back just enough to let me know he'd eased up.

"Hot damn, girl. That's some badass driving," Gran hooted.

My muscle memory had me anticipating the last turn even before I saw it. A benefit of having raced this track so many times before. The Jetta behind me was new. He was holding his own a lot better than I'd expected, but it wouldn't be enough.

I knew this course like the back of my hand.

Besides, after all the work Juice and I had done to this baby, that Jetta was no match for my Acura.

A sudden shove sent me lurching forward.

"What the—" Gran's wings buzzed as she was flung off the dash and barely caught air before being slammed into the window.

Outside, the sound of metal crunching had my eyes narrowing. I straightened, eyes darting to the rear mirror. The Jetta had dropped back and was coming in again.

"What in tarnation was that?" Gran demanded.

None of us had the heart to tell her "tarnation" wasn't

a curse word.

"Son of a. . ." I trailed off.

The jackwad had hit me.

On purpose.

My car lurched again.

This time, I felt my tires drift as the impact sent me sliding toward the far edge of the pavement. Dangerously close to the drop-off along the river.

"You little prick," I hissed.

Gran's wings beat wildly. "Oh, that little shitbrick is going down."

My fae senses took over, closing the gap between what a human could pull off and what my supernatural abilities allowed. I gripped the gear shift, downshifting as I punched the gas.

My back end swung out, kicking up gravel. I fishtailed before catching traction and straightening again. Veering left, I purposely clipped the Jetta's front end as I reclaimed my lead position.

"Watch and learn, you little shit."

"Yeah, watch and learn," Gran echoed. "You're no match for my granddaughter. She's the best in the damn state."

In my mirror, I watched the punk in the Jetta try to keep from losing control.

Aww. He could dish it out but he couldn't take it? I rolled my eyes. Then I slammed my foot against the gas and let my tires eat up the pavement. All that was left was a quarter mile straightaway now. I had him.

From the cupholder, my phone rang.

With one hand still on the wheel, I grabbed it and held it up.

The name *Vic Hawkins* flashed across the screen.

Shit.

"Who is it?" Gran asked.

"Dad."

"Ain't nobody got time for that," she said. "We'll call him back after we win. Make him buy us a victory drink."

I decided not to point out Gran couldn't consume more than a raindrop of alcohol without passing out. Instead, I dropped the phone back into the cupholder and eyed the Jetta right on my tail. My breath turned shallow with the need for victory.

Just ahead, the finish line was marked on each side by traffic cones Juice had snagged from a construction site nearby. We used whatever markers we could to keep from being noticed out here.

Beyond the cones, scantily clad girls stood on a pickup bed, waving their arms at us.

The Jetta's engine screamed in response.

In my cupholder, my phone pinged with a voice mail.

I sucked in a breath, squeezed the wheel, and forced myself not to use magic as my tires soared across the finish line.

Half a car length in front of the Jetta.

Punk.

"Yeah, baby! Fuck all the haters. Suck yo' momma's teats." Gran hooted and crowed our victory—not that any of the humans would pick up the sound.

Thank goodness.

Some of her insults got a little weird.

Pissed at what my opponent had tried out there, I braked hard, pulling to the left so that the front end whipped around in a tight U-turn. I slid to a stop, not even caring that I'd probably just stripped the remaining tread from my tires, and jumped out.

Gran started to follow, but I moved fast, not wanting to deal with her buzzing in my ear. Or worse, buzzing in someone else's. All it took was one well-placed hand swat and Gran was toast.

I couldn't have that kind of guilt on my conscience.

Slamming the door behind me, I shoved past the well-wishers all hooting and cheering my victory. Several of them knew me well enough and one look at my expression had them parting for me to pass.

On the other side of the crowd, the asshat in the Jetta slowed to a stop, his darkly tinted windows would have been impossible to see through if I'd been human.

I wasn't human. Not even close.

"Nice driving, G," someone called.

"Future champion of Bazemore, people, let her

through."

I ignored the comments from the regulars, glaring at the Jetta as I stalked closer.

"Get out of the car," I yelled, slamming my palm against his hood as I rounded the front end.

Several of the spectators followed, boxing me in between the Jetta and their nosy asses.

"What happened, G?" a male voice called from behind me.

Hector. Always up in people's business.

I ignored him and marched up to the driver's side door.

When the punk didn't open it, I lifted the handle and yanked the door wide. It squeaked on its hinges, and I had to stop myself from pulling it clean off.

"Whoa. You can't just—"

"What the hell was that?" I demanded.

A lanky guy with bad acne unfolded himself from the front seat. He towered over me by at least a foot, his expression somewhere between shocked and pouting.

"You could have killed me," I said. "Or yourself. Are you insane?"

He threw his hands up defensively.

"Whoa, lady. I don't know what you're talking about."

I stepped closer, unmoved by his innocent act. Inside, my fae magic mixed with the swirl of creatures I was capable of becoming. Every one of them was pissed and straining to get out.

"Don't play stupid with me," I hissed. "That kind of recklessness might work at your high school drag strip, but down here, we drive clean."

"Look, it was an accident, okay?"

"You ever touch my car again with so much as a dirty fingernail and I will rip your organs out of your asshole and—"

"Gem!"

Juice's voice was sharp.

I jerked toward the sound. "Give me a damn minute," I called.

"Now."

His tone was one I'd never heard before. That, more than the sniveling little schoolboy in front of me, had me stepping away.

"Get out of here," I told him, disgusted.

"Don't you want me to settle up with the bookie?" he asked, wide-eyed.

"I don't want your lunch money." I shoved past him and over to where Juice waited.

One look at his stricken expression and my stomach plummeted.

"What is it?" I asked. "Is it Z? Did he—?"

"Not Z," he said in a strained voice. Not that I could blame him. Z was my on again, off again boyfriend. Right now, we were off again, and Juice was thrilled.

"What then?"

Mine had been the only race so far, which meant no one else could have been injured. Not unless I changed my mind about the punk in the Jetta.

"It's your father." Juice's voice was gentle, but his words were so unexpected, I felt only confusion.

"My dad?" I frowned. "He's not even here tonight. You know he can't come to these. A conflict of interest."

"There was an accident, Gem."

I blinked. Thanks to the adrenaline still pumping through me, the words were taking longer than necessary to sink in.

"What kind of accident?"

Juice's mouth was drawn. "You should go home. Your mom is waiting for you so you can go downtown together."

A rushing sound rose up, blotting out the revving of engines behind me as the crowd began to disperse, heading back to the starting line for the next round.

"What kind of accident?" I repeated, voice rising.

Juice hesitated.

His eyes held the truth even before he managed to say the words.

"I'm so sorry. Your mom said the agency just called—"

"Juice, what happened?" I demanded.

"He's dead, Gem."

I didn't wait until he was finished before sprinting back to my car.

It was a mistake.

A terrible, horrible mistake.

He'd just called me not ten minutes ago.

Juice had bad information. I'd prove it.

Gran was already ranting when I slid into the car and shut the door behind me. Ignoring her, I grabbed my phone, hand trembling.

"Gem? What is it, honey?" Gran demanded. "Who are you calling?"

I didn't answer.

With a couple quick swipes, I dialed my father. It rang and rang before finally going to voice mail.

"You've reached Vic Hawkins. I'm busy. You know what to do."

He sounded gruff, an attempt at "tough cop" that had made my mother and I tease him for days. My dad wasn't gruff. Not on two legs anyway. His griffin side was another story, but that was a form he used for good. Everything about my dad was pure light.

My hands and feet went cold as the truth of Juice's words finally sunk in. I hung up without leaving a message and looked down at my phone. My eyes caught on the notification I'd ignored before. I had a voice mail.

"Gem?" Gran's tone was more urgent now. More worried.

"One second," I whispered.

Juice walked up, his expression wary and full of empathy.

I hit the button to lower my window.

"Gem, go to your mom," Juice said gently. "She needs you to go downtown. To identify his—"

"Don't say it."

Part of me still wanted to believe this was all a terrible mistake. Someone had decided to play a prank. Or maybe he'd just been injured. But deep in my gut, I couldn't shake the throbbing pain that grew steadily bigger as it wiped out the doubt.

Juice didn't try to stop me as I started the engine and threw the car into reverse. Squealing tires, I backed up and then slammed it into first, peeling out as I headed for the main road.

"Dammit, Gemma-girl, tell me what's happening right now," Gran demanded.

I didn't answer. I couldn't. If losing Grandpa Cal had forced Gran into this form, what would losing her son do?

In my rearview, Juice watched me go, sad and solitary in the darkness.

Refusing to let my emotions take me over, I kept my eyes on the road as steadily as if this were another race. At the finish line, my parents would be waiting, my father's happy smile the prize.

He had to be okay.

He had to be alive.

I didn't want to imagine what I'd do if he was gone.

TWO

They called it a fluke. Some prick of a demon—level one supposedly—had caught him off guard while out on patrol. Vic Hawkins. The most decorated agent in the entire Supernatural Security Force. The supe who'd vanquished more demons in his career than any other agent on the force. Maybe he'd been distracted, they said. All I could think about was that phone call I'd ignored.

For four days, my mother and I camped out at headquarters while she sat through debriefs and questioning about Dad's last days. He'd left notes about a "big find" and a "demon problem unlike any we've ever seen." No one knew what it meant, but all the higher-ups treated us like criminals for the questions those notes raised. No one seemed to care that while they'd lost their best agent, my mother had lost her mate. Fae took a hit like that especially hard.

By day five, I saw the process for what it was: an interrogation. When I realized it, I marched in with Gran in my pocket and took my mother home.

The funeral arrangements had been handled for us with no consideration for what we wanted. For what Dad would have wanted.

Human heroes who were killed by the enemy got a flag and a twenty-one gun salute. The supes in charge of sending my dad off into the Great Beyond had given us a racist preacher with a reputation for inciting violence against anything non-human. The fact that they'd selected a priest who clearly knew about our kind and despised us despite the good we did for humans made my rage even worse.

Maybe I'd wake up one day and find I'd become a June bug too.

So far, though, I was still me. Gem Hawkins, daughter to the deceased, granddaughter to a mourning beetle, the only creature in this world my mother trusted—and all of us were being watched. During the processional from the church to the cemetery, I told myself the sensation of eyes on my back stemmed from the other mourners hoping to get a first-row seat to my meltdown. But by the time the priest had begun reciting the twenty-third Psalm, I knew it was more than that.

When we all stood to sing "Amazing Grace," I glanced over my shoulder.

There.

A dark suit half-hidden behind a tree several yards to my left.

As my gaze swung back to the priest, I faltered.

Another suit. Huddled behind a mausoleum decked out in cherub sculptures. And when I twisted to take in a full scan of the parking lot, three more.

Agents.

Because apparently ridding the city of demons wasn't as much of a priority as spying at a funeral. Why the hell they felt the need to hide was a mystery.

My mother's sniffles called me back, and I straightened, tightening my grip around her waist. Around us, the guests murmured the lyrics, and my mother's lip trembled as she tried to join them. From inside my mother's purse, Gran sniffled too.

I glared at the priest who'd ignored my song choice in favor of the hymn we all sung now. He met my eyes and smiled tightly, then finished out the song. At his direction, we all sat again, and he launched into some diatribe about the dangers of cavorting with demons on a daily basis.

"I'll give that assmuncher something to cavort with."

Gran's voice at my ear startled me.

"Ssh," I told her, eyes on the priest still ranting passive-aggressively at our kind.

Beside me, his wife, a plump human woman with a

shrill voice, patted my hand as if to remind me not to end up like the deceased.

It took every ounce of self-control I had not to shift right in front of her. I'd go with a giant worm or maybe a slug. Something with lots of slime and goo. Picturing her reaction when she saw what I could become was a small comfort.

"Corinthians says, 'But the sacrifices of pagans are offered to demons, not to God, and I do not want you to participate with demons.'" The priest shot me and my mother a pointed glare. "You cannot drink the cup of the Lord and the cup of the demons too. You cannot have a part in both the Lord's table and the table of the demons."

"I'm gonna pray for him," Gran muttered.

This time I didn't shush her.

This funeral was bullshit. Fake people using fake words to convey a fake sense of comfort. The only real thing amid the mountains of roses and somber-faced agents was my mother's sniffles. Even those were muffled for propriety's sake. Screw propriety. I was stone-faced, and not because I wasn't crushed. My grieving just happened to contain a deep layer of rage I hadn't yet found the bottom of. And if Gran's mutterings were any indication, I wasn't alone in my rage.

While Gran mumbled about "the vengeance of the Lord," I focused instead on the smooth walnut finish of the casket.

It was half-covered by a cloth adorned with the seal of the Nephilim. A symbol of the strength that had failed the one man it should have stopped at nothing to save. The Supernatural Security Force had let him die on duty, and his murderer was still out there. While all of them sat here, doing not a damn thing about it. Well, unless you counted footing the bill for funeral decor one might find on the clearance aisle.

It was a slap in the face. One I hoped my mother hadn't caught on to.

Finally, the priest finished his lecture and instructed everyone to bow their heads. I lowered my chin, and the back of my neck prickled. Glancing sideways, I paused at the sight of a figure along the edge of the looping driveway that bordered the burial sites.

Even from here, I could tell he was male.

Broad shoulders, dark hair, and fiercely intent on our little gathering. He wasn't in a suit like the other lackeys. And he didn't scan the area for unseen threats like the others did.

I blinked, using my fae senses to hone in. His face was still too shadowed to make out, but his eyes—those were sharp and mysterious and, if I wasn't mistaken, locked on me.

What the hell? Who would come all this way just to watch from the tree line?

Z maybe, but the mysterious stranger lurking at the

fringe wasn't Z. He had a different sort of energy about him. Less slick. More . . . dangerous.

Besides, Z was currently not returning my texts. Jerk.

The prayer ended.

Fabric shuffled as the priest dismissed us and the guests began to rise.

Gran returned to my mother's purse to wait it out. My mom took a steadying breath, and I turned my attention back to her as we rose to meet the well-wishers coming to pay their respects.

The next few minutes were filled with murmured reassurances and careful hugs. Some of the faces were familiar: our neighbor Carmen, who sometimes played bingo with Mom. Lila from the sandwich shop where I'd worked for the past four years. And Juice, my mechanic.

"Hey, girl." He pulled me into a one-armed hug then hugged my mom more gently.

"Thank you for coming," she said.

"Vic was a good guy," he told her.

She offered a watery smile and patted his arm.

"Call me later," he told me.

I nodded, and he walked off slowly, hands stuffed into his hoodie.

Beyond the few friends, most were strangers to me. Acquaintances and friends of my parents. My dad's bowling buddies.

Finally, the crowd began to thin.

"Cora," a male voice called out.

The line of well-wishers had dwindled until the strange man smiling down at my mother was the only one left. Beyond him, a small army of suits stood scattered around. Every one of them watched our exchange like we might take him out at any moment. Agency guys. Which meant the suit before me was someone important.

Good. Maybe he had answers.

I noted the dark eyes and hard features that made up his handsome face. Attractive but dangerous. My magic crackled at his proximity, and I fought the urge to step between him and my mother.

"I'm so sorry for your loss."

She smiled tightly back and let him take her hand. "Thank you, Raph. It's good to see you."

"I only wish it were under better circumstances."

She didn't offer an answer, only paled at the mention of what had brought us together.

He brushed his lips across her hand then released it, turning to me. "You must be Gemini. Your father spoke highly of you."

The weight of his gaze rooted me.

"Gem, this is Raphziel," my mother said quietly. "He worked with your father."

Raphziel smiled in a way that made my stomach tighten.

I shook his offered hand and shuddered at the zing of power that came with his touch.

Something in his eyes flickered.

Raw power.

Nephilim, I realized, dazed by it.

I'd never touched one before. Never been this close. No wonder my magic was on high alert. I could practically smell the otherworldliness of him.

"Your father was a good man," he said.

The words were enough to wake me up; remind me why we were really here. Who Raphziel really was.

"Does that mean you're going to catch who killed him?"

"Gem," my mother whispered. "Now's not exactly the time."

"Girl's got a point, Cora."

Raph's forehead crinkled in confusion as he searched for the source of the voice.

My mother's face flushed. She gestured to the purse.

"My mother-in-law is—"

"Tired of the bull shrimp," Gran said menacingly.

Or as menacingly as a June bug could be.

My mother looked horrified, but Raph shook his head.

"It's fine, Cora. Of course you all want answers. So do we." He turned back to me, his expression bland as if placating a child. "The investigation is ongoing, which means I can't say much, but we're doing everything we can."

"Not everything," I said, and he frowned.

"Excuse me?"

"There was a witness. I read about it in the report the coroner shared with us."

His eyes narrowed then smoothed again. "The witness information was redacted."

"I un-redacted it." With magic. I left that part out.

When he didn't answer, I pressed on.

"Anyway, like I said, there's a witness, but no one has located him or her. Maybe if more resources were diverted to finding whoever this person is, we'd get a lead."

"Unfortunately, the witness you read about was the victim of a rata demon two nights ago."

"How convenient."

The Nephilim's smile turned sharp.

Behind him, a couple of the goons took a step closer, and I realized even my small push back was more than Raphziel was used to allowing.

"Your enthusiasm for the investigation is admirable, Miss Hawkins. I can assure you we have our best agents already working around the clock to track down the demon who did this."

I didn't bother putting words to the fact that there'd been zero evidence on his body of a demon being the murderer. Demons ripped or clawed or chewed. Not a trace of any of those things was visible when we'd gone to identify him. And according to the coroner's report—also magically unredacted by yours truly—there hadn't been a mark on him when he'd been found. But clearly, the SSF had already made up its mind about what they wanted to believe—or wanted us to believe.

Raphziel was no exception.

"Cora, why don't you let my men escort you home? You look exhausted after today's service. I hope it wasn't too much, but we wanted to do everything we could to help lay Vic to rest."

"Who could rest with that priest railing on against abominations?" Gran said.

I gave Raph a hard look. "The service was—"

"Beautiful," my mother said, cutting me off.

She shot me a look.

"I'm so glad you enjoyed it," Raphziel said.

I bit back another angry reply. Who the hell enjoyed a funeral? Especially one where the priest acted like I was the evil that was wrong the world?

"It was unforgettable," I said instead.

Gran snorted. "A shart is unforgettable too."

Raphziel motioned at his goons, who started toward his black SUV like some sort of angry suit parade.

"I'm so glad we could be there for you in this time of need," he said. "Cora, why don't you let me drive you home? You look absolutely destroyed and in no shape to be driving."

He tried leading my mother away, but I grabbed her hand.

"That's okay. I drove, so we'll just take our own vehicle. Luckily, I can drive while looking like shit."

"Gem," my mother scolded.

Gran snickered.

Raphziel's smile turned cold, but I was over it, Nephilim or not. They'd controlled my dad's entire life. I wasn't going to let them control his death too.

"You have our number if there's any new information," I added.

My mother didn't protest as I dragged her away from the Nephilim.

I could feel Raph's eyes on our backs as we went, and I knew better than to say a word until we were out of the cemetery and safely in the car. Thankfully, Gran had gone quiet too. Or mostly. The occasional grumble about "untrustworthy angels of darkness" broke through but otherwise, she let it go.

"I can't believe he just blew us off about the investigation *and* told us we look like shit," I said after slamming my door closed.

"You challenged a Nephilim, Gem, what did you expect?"

"A step above assholery, maybe?" I gripped the steering

wheel and jammed the key into the ignition. "I mean, today of all days, they could grow some manners, right? They didn't even stick to our wishes for the service arrangements."

My mother sighed. "You're talking about Nephilim. And Raph, at that. He's not exactly known for his kindness and tact."

"He's an ass."

"He's an ass*monkey*," Gran put in.

My mother winced. "He was your father's boss," she said pointedly.

I glanced over and saw something in her expression. "Wait. In the report, it said his superior was the one who sent him out solo that night. That was Raph's call?"

"Raph made a lot of calls your father didn't like," my mother said in a strained voice.

Of course he did.

"Fucking Nephilim," Gran muttered. "Always acting like they know better."

She wasn't wrong. I had a feeling Raph's promises about answers were bullshit, just like their attempts to comfort us had been so far. Hiring a human priest who hated supes? Rage boiled in my veins, threatening to unleash my inner beast, but I forced it down.

Losing my shit on such a terrible day wouldn't do anyone any good. I had to be smart.

"I know that look," Mom said. I glanced over to see her watching me warily. "What are you thinking?"

"That we need to go home," I told her, turning the key and starting the engine.

She sighed. "Good. I'm sure the neighbors will want to stop by to pay their respects—"

"Fuck those lintlickers," Gran said.

"Please don't say that to Luca Diablo," my mother said, swiping a hand over her face.

"I ain't scared of him," Gran muttered.

My mom shot me a pleading look, probably hoping I'd help tone Gran down. But my mind was elsewhere as I pulled out of the cemetery. In the rearview, I tracked Raph and his cavalcade of agency minions as they drove off in the opposite direction.

"Let the Diablo pack come," I said. "I want to talk to them anyway."

"Why?" Mom sounded legit worried now.

"You heard Raph today," I told her. "And the other agents at headquarters this past week. They're acting like Dad was dirty or something, and they're not doing shit to find out what really happened to him. I for one am not going to sit around while the real killer gets away."

"What are you going to do, hire the Diablo pack to investigate?" Mom asked. We all knew the Diablos weren't exactly ethical.

"Yeah. We need to bust a cap," Gran said.

"No, I'm going to ask Luca for advice." I glanced down at the purse where Gran was still hanging out. "We need to make a plan," I told her. "Dad would have insisted on strategy above all else."

"Gem's right, Cora," Gran said. She flew up and landed on the dashboard so she could look my mother in the eye. "Vic deserves justice."

Silence followed.

"All right," my mother finally said, and Gran flew in circles, chattering about "those twatwaffle Neph going down."

My mother made the sign of the cross—which was weird considering we weren't religious. Gran was clearly driving her to desperation.

While I drove, I let my thoughts wander toward a plan of some kind. My usual tactic was to rush in and bulldoze over whoever got in my way. I'd grown up in a neighborhood of gangster werewolves where brawns, not brains, ruled. Luca Diablo was the closest thing to the Godfather I'd ever met. Playtime with him and his cousins had consisted of a never-ending game of "cops and robbers," only no one had the guts to be the cop once Luca got done with them.

Between that and my penchant for speed, I'd gotten myself into more than one sticky situation thanks to my lack of patience and planning. But this time, Gran was right. I'd honor Dad by being smart about this, by forming a plan that would stand up against whatever conspiracy was covering up the truth about his death. And then I'd avenge him by carrying it out.

THREE

The sound of revving engines hit me long before I saw the cars. Rounding the corner, the warehouses gave way to an open lot and a convergence of rice rockets and muscle cars that could only mean one thing. Tonight was race night. Normally, I arrived as part of the turbo-charged processional. Tonight, however, I'd already parked and glamoured my baby for safekeeping. I couldn't afford to be spotted at an illegal race. Not even by the human police. There was too much at stake for that kind of risk.

For this plan to work, I had to keep my nose clean.

Approaching on foot, my worn jacket didn't do much to keep me warm against the night breeze coming off the water. Rather than dwell on what I was about to do to my team, I fantasized about the leather jacket I'd seen at Shepherd's last week. It would have been a hell of a lot warmer than this one, but I couldn't spare the extra cash. Not when my last shift was tomorrow.

Up ahead, people milled around in the darkness. The streetlights had been knocked out to preserve anonymity, but I recognized the ratty tee and squared shoulders as he bent over an open hood.

"Juice."

My mechanic looked up, his mustache nearly blending with his dark coloring.

"Gem." He gave me a quick kiss on the cheek and a one-armed hug. "How's your mom?"

"She's good. Home with Gran."

He nodded. "Tell them both I send my regards."

Juice wasn't the only human who knew about supes. But he was the only one who'd managed to earn the trust of my entire family—and therefore knew the secret of what Gran really was.

Dad had liked Juice. He'd appreciated the lack of questions. Questions had always made it hard to live among humans, but not with Juice. He just accepted us. Said *who* you were mattered more than *what* you were.

"We got some new equipment tonight?" I asked, gesturing to the Japanese import he was checking out.

A guy with a bandanna stood close, eyeing me suspiciously. I hadn't seen him around, but new didn't mean amateur. People came from all over to challenge us. Okay, me.

Or they used to.

"Carl here thinks he can hang with the big girls," Juice said.

"Don't you mean big *boys*?" a husky guy with glasses asked. He stood near the car Juice had been checking out, and I could only assume he was some kind of wingman.

I glared at him, but Juice was the one to snap, "Around here it's the female who does the ass-kicking. You got a problem with that?"

"No problem," Carl, the skinny bandanna said. He glanced at me. "I can hang."

"Hmm." I eyed his setup but remained quiet while Juice finished his perusal.

Finally, he slammed the hood closed and pulled a dirty rag from his back pocket, wiping his grease-stained hands. Around us, voices rose as more of the regulars arrived for tonight's events.

We had everything; from rice rockets built out of Mom's allowance to supercars custom ordered with trust fund money. No judgment from me. It didn't matter where your car came from or even what kind it was. Out here, all that mattered was you could drive worth a shit. If you couldn't, you were either left in the dust or, in a very worst case scenario that had only happened once, taking a fast dip into the Mississippi.

I loved how the roads never cared about things like class and money.

"Well?" Carl demanded when Juice remained silent.

Juice shot me a look then leveled his gaze at the new kid. "It's not terrible," he said finally.

I hid a smile. It was the closest Carl would get to a compliment, whether he knew it or not.

"What does that mean?" Carl asked. "Can I race or not?"

"Sure, why not? Manny's sick, and I'm one short."

Carl's eyes lit up. "Sweet."

"Get your ass moving, though. You're up next." Carl said it lightly, but I knew better. If he was putting Carl in, Juice saw something in him. Good for me, since I was about to leave Juice without his best driver.

"Cool." Carl hopped in and started his car, angling it toward the small opening that would take him onto the empty strip.

"He ever raced before?" I asked Juice as we watched him get into position.

"His brother is Billy Fresh."

I lifted my brows. "Damn. Well okay then. Hopefully the apple didn't fall far."

"We'll see." Juice sounded neutral, but I knew better. I'd seen that gleam in his eye before. He was hoping this kid had something.

I also knew now wasn't the time to drop my little bomb.

"Go get a better seat," I told him. "I'll find you later."

He grunted and began cutting through the crowd. A few bystanders spotted me and waved. I waved back then cut behind them until I'd lost sight of familiar faces. Normally, I'd hang near the front with Juice, but tonight, I didn't want to get roped into any conversations that required more lies.

"Gem."

I looked up and immediately wished I'd gone with Juice after all. Dammit. This was one goodbye I'd hoped to avoid.

"I thought you weren't coming tonight," I said.

Sparkly blue eyes shone back at me in the darkness. His were slanted thanks to his distant Asian heritage—an ethnicity that only made him more handsome. Perfect skin. Perfect eyes. At least his warlock skills were only mediocre.

"I wanted to see you."

I bit back a sigh. "Lucky me."

His half-smile, a signature look for him, dimmed. "You're not happy to see me?"

"We talked about this."

"We didn't talk. We texted."

And whose fault was that?

"Taking a break means getting some space for a while," I reminded him.

He stepped closer. "I've had enough space."

The scent of his cologne washed over me, and I tried to hold my breath. That smell had the power to make me stupid. As did those hands and that mouth. But the eyes. Those were the worst.

And right now those eyes were practically undressing me.

His hands landed on my hips. His mouth brushed close to my cheek as he bent low. "Space is overrated," he said quietly.

Sexily.

Dammit.

"Z, I can't," I said, while wondering if I actually could. But no. That would be a bad idea.

"I haven't asked you to do anything yet."

"Your eyes are asking. So are your hands."

He chuckled, and for some reason that triggered common sense. Maybe because the last time I'd heard him chuckle, it had been at the idea of me ever being anything more than an amateur drag race driver.

Asshole.

I stepped back, and this time when I looked up at him, those eyes didn't do shit for my lady parts.

"What's wrong?"

"We're done, Z. Over."

"I know, you said you needed a break."

"No break. This is permanent."

"You don't mean that. Gemmy, we're good together." He stepped closer again. "Our bodies are good together."

"That might have been true for a while but not

anymore. Starting right now, this body is good without you. Better, in fact."

"Gemmy."

His stupid nickname grated on me.

"Did you know my dad died?"

"I . . ."

He hesitated. Of course he knew. I'd texted him days ago and nothing. Until tonight, when he decided he was horny.

Ugh. Warlocks were jerks. Okay, maybe it was just Z.

"I'm so sorry for your loss, Gemmy. I didn't text you back because I just didn't know what to say."

My patience broke.

"I'm leaving, Z. For good. After tonight, I won't be back."

His eyes widened. "You're giving up driving?"

"I'm moving on," I said with emphasis.

He studied me like he couldn't decide whether or not to worry.

"If this is about trying to go pro, I want you to know—"

"This has nothing to do with you, Z. Which is why I don't owe you an explanation. Just clarity. We're done. Have a nice life."

My temper had me marching off without looking.

Z let me go—what else did I expect, really? But I hadn't gone far when I bumped a shoulder I hadn't noticed in the dark. Z had shaken me more than I wanted to admit if my fae senses hadn't picked out the human in my path.

"You're done?"

Juice's voice was low with surprise, but underneath that, he sounded hurt.

Shit.

"I was going to tell you after the race," I said, shoulders sagging underneath the guilt. "I didn't mean for you to hear it that way."

I glanced back but already Z was gone, vanished into the crowd and probably already hunting for another lady friend who would succumb to his sweet talk.

"I always knew you'd get out," Juice said, and I blinked in surprise.

"You're not mad?"

"You're not a lifer, kid. I can't be mad at that. There's something better waiting for you."

"I don't know about *better*," I said.

And because it was Juice, and because he'd become like a second father to me, at least as far as the roads were concerned, I told him everything right down to my plan to get answers.

When I was done, he whistled. "Shit, Gem. That's a lot. You sure you want to do this?"

"My father deserves justice," I said.

He nodded. "I hear that." He glanced back at the

sound of engines revving at the line. The crowd was cheering loudly enough that I wasn't worried about being overheard. "You can't come back here," he added sadly. "After."

"I know."

Sadness hit me like a weight. I was seriously going to miss this scene.

"Come by my shop, though," he said, and hope returned.

"Really?"

He squeezed my shoulder. "You're family, Gem. Come see me anytime." His smile turned sly. "Just not here. Because I'll be damned if I let you arrest me."

I laughed. "Relax, old man. You're just a lowly human. Not even on my radar."

He snorted. "Can't say I'm sorry about that."

Juice knew about supes though I could never get him to tell me what led him to the discovery. He had an uncanny way about sensing magic in others, though. He'd known what Z was in less than five minutes. And not just the womanizer player type either.

"Thanks for being cool, Juice. I'll stop by the shop when I can."

"Be safe, girl."

I gave him a quick hug and then started down the alley, circling the crowd to avoid anyone else who might demand an explanation I wasn't in the mood to give.

"Hey Gem," Juice called to my back.

"Yeah?"

"Carl Fresh can drive but he ain't got shit on you."

I smiled. "Damn right he doesn't."

FOUR

I waved at the last two customers as they left, and then slumped against the counter. My feet hurt and my thighs ached from standing for so many hours straight. Exhaustion made me cranky. Hunger made me whiny. Not a great combination.

"Ugh. If I never make another sandwich again, I'll die happy," I groaned.

From the other end of the counter, Lila offered a wry smirk before tossing a dishrag at me. "Not anytime soon, though, I hope. Your country needs you. Isn't that the slogan?"

I stuck my tongue out at her. "That's the human military, smartass."

"Oh, right. Your *species* needs you. That's it." She gave me a mock salute. "The few. The proud. The demon killers."

I shook my head and went to work wiping everything down so we could close up.

Lila's Sandwich Shop was located on the cusp of the French Quarter, so we saw all kinds. Drunk, sober, human, supe—I'd served them all in the five years I'd worked here. All in all, aside from that one incident involving the food chopper, it had been a fun job while it lasted.

"You're just salty about losing your guinea pig," I told her.

She laughed. "Of course I am. Who else is going to test out my pickled okra and goat cheese panini?"

"Pickled okra? Lila, gross."

"You say that now, but it could be genius. Remember the olive and peanut butter croissant?"

"Remember the pastrami and jerk sauce on blueberry scone?" I shot back.

"Ugh. Why do you always bring up the losers?"

I shuddered at the memory of that particular taste combination. "I can't help it. Sandwich PTSD is real."

She tossed another dishrag at me. It hit me in the shoulder and left a wet spot that I hoped was only water on the front of my ribbed tank.

"Whatever. It's better than demon combat," she said.

"Don't be so sure."

Lila's aunt had been killed by a mud demon several years back. Ever since, Lila had made it a point to confront the supernatural underbelly that existed under every human's nose. She was pretty good with weird and crazy, which made our friendship work when my others hadn't.

"Here."

Lila handed me a package, and I frowned.

"What's this?"

"It's called a present, genius. Open it."

I pulled back the outer wrapping and ran my hands over the soft purple leather inside.

"Lila," I began.

She grinned. "Put it on."

I slid my arms into the leather jacket, and Lila whistled.

"Definitely demon slayer material."

"It's the jacket from Shepherd's. The one I wanted to wear for Bazemore."

Bazemore was the biggest event for drag racers in the state. It came once a year, and I'd been training for it forever. After three years of competing, my record was number two in the state. A title I'd planned to improve upon, until Dad had been killed and his murderer left to roam free.

She shrugged. "Maybe you still will someday. For now, you can break it in while slaying monsters or whatever."

My eyes burned, but I refused to cry. "This is the nicest thing anyone's ever done for me. You can't afford this."

"Of course I can't. So don't come around for free lunches or anything. SSF pays full price."

I snorted. "Fair. And, Lila, thanks."

She bumped my shoulder. "Break a leg, champ. In fact, sever limbs while you're at it. Demon limbs, I mean. Not yours."

"Don't worry. If I meet one I can't kill, I'll bring him in for a sandwich."

"That's it, you're fired."

I laughed.

It took an hour to close up, and another forty minutes for my going-away drink. By the time I headed home in my new leather jacket, I was feeling loose and a little less rage-y than usual.

The past three months had cooled the worst of it, but my desire for vengeance hadn't budged. Thanks to watching my mom grieve her mate, it had only grown stronger.

Now it was all I thought about.

Head down, collar up, I walked the four blocks from Lila's to my mother's house. Despite the late hour, music and laughter spilled out of the bars I passed. The scent of sweat and alcohol mixed with the undercurrent of magic. Humans lived side by side with supes, and still they only saw what they wanted to.

I couldn't blame them. If I could turn a blind eye to all

the things that kept me awake at night, I would do it in a heartbeat.

Unfortunately, there was no escaping reality. Not for me. Tomorrow, though. Tomorrow, I'd step into a new one. Phase one of the plan.

Tonight, I'd toast my old life goodbye.

Halfway home, my steps slowed as the sensation of eyes on my back settled between my shoulder blades.

I'd felt it more than once since that day at the cemetery. Each time was the same feeling of being watched. But whenever I tried to spot my stalker, there was no one there.

Turning a sharp corner, I glanced behind me.

A hand shot out, yanking my sleeve until I spun and landed hard against the building at my back.

"What—"

"Shut up and listen," a rough voice said.

Hot breath hit my cheek as whoever had grabbed me leaned in close. The smell of aftershave hit my nose. I inhaled, trying to identify it, but the smell and stance of the man was foreign to me.

Not human.

Not fae.

Shifter, my senses told me. Not wolf. Something else.

"I know what you're trying to do," he hissed. "And it won't work."

"I'm not doing anything," I said, anger building as my

store of creatures gathered underneath my skin. "Unless you count walking home."

The hands around my collar tightened until my breath caught.

"What's done is done. Digging it up will only cause more problems. Don't show up tomorrow. Go back to making sandwiches. Or you'll regret it."

Quickly, I chose a creature. It rose to the surface, transforming my skin from human flesh to thick fur. My fingers became sharp claws. My predator nature took over, and the tiger I'd become lashed out.

I snapped my teeth at the stranger pinning me but the weight of him vanished before I could bite him. A ripple of wind tousled my fur and then he was gone.

Adrenaline pumping, I dropped to all fours and prowled the alley. The smell of aftershave lingered but the man was gone. His scent untraceable in the wet night air.

Damn.

On a snarl, I backed into the darkest corner and let my tiger fade until I was me again.

My mind raced, trying to understand what had just happened. Clearly, my becoming an agent was threatening to someone. Was it someone on the inside? Who else other than the SSF knew I was reporting in tomorrow?

The more I thought about the stranger, the more questions I had for him. Trying to follow his trail was useless, though. He was just . . . gone. His trail vanished right where he'd pinned me. It didn't make sense.

I hurried home, all the while keeping my fae senses open for some sign of another ambush.

But there was nothing.

I was alone in the night.

Finally, I turned and headed for my mother's house.

ON THE PORCH, I paused and opened my senses before entering the two-story townhouse I'd grown up in. The energy coating the place had always been strange thanks to the unusual mix of fae and shifter magic wound around the place like some kind of supernatural barbed wire fence. But this was different. Almost immediately, angry magic prickled my skin, and I looked up just as a large hammer blinked into existence and swung at me in a downward arc.

I yelped and jumped back, narrowly avoiding getting smashed in the face.

The hammer winked away, and I was left alone in the dark, hands on my knees, trying to breathe through the heart attack I was fighting off.

The screen door creaked as it opened a few inches.

I looked up at my mother peering out the small opening.

When she saw me, her eyes widened.

"Gem, what the hell. I thought you were a prowler."

"Nope. Just me. Your one and only daughter. Almost beheaded by your alarm system."

"I'm so sorry." She pushed open the door, and I straightened, sliding past her into the house.

My mother leaned out, darting glances left and right into the empty street.

"There's no one else out there," I told her, knowing how paranoid she'd been these last few months. "Also, no one says prowler anymore."

I looked back to see her eyes cast to the ceiling. Her lips moved in silent muttering, and I hid a smile.

"Look, if you just call or text me next time, I can disable the alarm system."

"And lose out on the chance to test its effectiveness?" I scoffed. "No way."

My mom gave me a look that said she wasn't amused.

"Besides, I did call. This morning. Remember? I told you I'd come by for a nightcap when I was done at Lila's?"

Her eyes widened. "Oh, crap. You did call. I totally forgot."

"It's okay." I leaned in to drop a kiss on her cheek. "You have a lot on your mind."

She didn't answer. Grief had hit her heavily these last

few weeks. Dark circles ringed her eyes, and thanks to Gran's reports, I knew she was barely sleeping.

"Where's Gran?" I asked.

"She went down to Marlene's for Bingo."

"How the hell is she going to play Bingo? She doesn't even have hands."

Mom shrugged. "She says she likes to watch the old men fight about how their arthritis made their reflexes too slow to mark their winning squares."

I lifted a brow. "Has Gran always been a gangster and Grandpa Cal just kept her in check?"

"What do you think?"

"I think if she was still on two legs, she'd be in prison."

Mom snorted.

"What's for dinner?" I asked, heading for the kitchen.

"It's nearly midnight. You haven't eaten dinner?"

The tone was one I knew well: worry and chastisement. My mom had a gift for multitasking parental emotions.

"I ate first dinner with Lila. Now, I want second dinner. Got anything good?"

I didn't wait for an answer before yanking open the fridge and digging around. I came away with potato salad and carafels—a fae delicacy my mother sometimes made when she was missing her family.

I dug into the container, not bothering with a fork.

When I looked up, mouth overflowing, my mother was watching me with arms folded and brows raised.

"Manners, young lady," she said.

I decided to let that argument go. We both knew I got my manners from dad.

"You all ready for tomorrow?" she asked when I'd adjusted to more ladylike bites.

"More than ready," I assured her. "I got this."

Her brows scrunched with worry. I decided to leave out the part about the goon in the alley just now. She was already worried enough, and his threats only made me want this more.

"You don't have to do this, you know," she began, and I cut her off, too sick of the same old argument to indulge her tonight.

"I do, Mom. And you know it." I set the food aside. "The time for talking me out of it is long gone. Save your breath and just keep the carafels coming, okay?"

"Gem, I'm your mother. I'll always talk you out of stuff that could get you killed."

"Please." I rolled my eyes. "You sent me on a playdate with the Diablo pack when I was six."

She waved a dismissive hand. "Bah. I knew you could handle those wimps."

I grinned.

She smiled.

It wobbled.

"Pretend all the other recruits are the Diablo pack," I said.

She arched a brow. "It's not the recruits I'm worried about."

"The instructors," I said knowingly.

I'd done my research and already knew who to watch for. But I wasn't going to tell her any of the dirt. It would only make things worse.

"Your father told me his time at the academy was the worst of his career," she warned. "And he said it was nothing compared to how they treated the kids whose parents had been agents. Those trainers live for making your life hell. Once they find out you're a legacy, they might decide to go harder."

"I can handle it," I insisted, but the fact that she'd broken her own rule and mentioned Dad meant she was seriously worried for me.

"Your magic—"

"Is a secret," I finished. "I know, Mom. You and Dad spent my entire life drilling it into me. No one knows I can shapeshift."

Shapeshifters had all but vanished from the supernatural community in the last few decades. No one knew why or where they'd been taken, but the mystery only made it more dangerous. Dad had spent countless hours with me over the years, teaching me how to hide my ability. And

Gran had apologized more than once for unwittingly passing on that part of her DNA to mine.

Even now, anyone who asked about Gran's strange transformation got a story about how some witch had cursed her. It was safer than the truth.

"Use your griffin," Mom urged. "It's safest."

Because it was my father's form. We'd let everyone believe it was my only form too. I hadn't been able to bring myself to take his form since he'd died, but now wasn't the time to tell her that. She needed to think I could be strong.

"I know," I said gently, wishing I didn't have to leave her alone.

My mother stared back at me. "You're the only family I have left." Rather than sadness or fear, fury gleamed in her fae eyes. "I won't let anyone hurt you."

"No one would dare," I said. "Not with you backing me."

Magic glimmered behind her rage, and I nearly smiled at the feel of it filling the room between us. I'd never met a more powerful fae than my mom. I'd also never met a creature more protective. Combine those two and no bully had ever stood a chance against me. I was lucky, though. She hadn't used it to coddle me. Instead, she'd forged me.

I was daddy's girl, but I was Momma's warrior.

And tomorrow, I'd use both of those elements to follow in the footsteps of the only man who'd ever loved us both.

"Come on," I said, linking my arm through hers and

guiding her back to the living room. "Let's drink bourbon and watch reruns of *Buffy*. I'm in the mood for a Spike and Angel sandwich tonight."

"I thought you were done with sandwiches," she said, amusement gleaming.

"You're not wrong. But I think for those two, I'll always make an exception."

FIVE

Wind whipped, unforgiving and sharp, as I made my way through the wet streets. New Orleans was either brutally hot or bone-chillingly soaked—there were no in-betweens. Today, bone-chilling seemed more apt anyway. I'd slept like shit thanks to last night's mysterious stalker. Not that I'd been hurt when he'd grabbed me, but there'd been a vague promise for pain later if I reported in today. I'd already done what I could to secure my apartment. And encouraged my mother to reset her own booby traps. But if some lackey at the SSF thought shoving me around in an alley was going to stop me, he was sadly mistaken. If anything, it only made me more determined.

I walked with my head down and arms crossed tight in my new leather jacket, hoping my car was still safe when I got out of here. There was nowhere to store it on this side of town. Nowhere that wouldn't result in four missing tires when I completed my three-month training program, anyway. I'd left it at my mother's and made her promise to glamour it while I was gone.

"Wait . . . up."

Gran's voice was interrupted by a buzzy-sounding wheeze.

I slowed as Gran flew up and landed-slash-fell into my open palm.

"Shiznit, you walk fast," she said, huffing.

"I walk like a person with legs," I told her.

She glared up at me with her bug eyes. "Don't sass me, girl."

"Gran, I have to get going or I'll be late."

"I just wanted to wish you luck. Give those SSF lintlickers a run for their money."

"I'll do my best."

"You break up with that warlock yet?"

"Z and I are over, yes."

"Good." She huffed. "That asscracker isn't nearly good enough for you."

"Gran."

"What?"

"No one says asscracker."

"I'm startin' a trend."

I shook my head. "I really need to go."

Wings fluttered and Gran lifted off, hovering at eye

level as she stared back at me. "I love you, kid. Make me proud."

"Love you too, Gran. Take care of Mom for me, and don't get eaten before I get back."

"I'd like to see a motherfather try," she said before buzzing away.

When she was gone, I hooked my bag higher on my shoulder and continued on.

As I got closer, my senses prickled, alert and wary.

Twice, I jerked my head upward to scan the rooftops. The hair on my neck stood up, and I was positive someone up there was tracking my journey. But when I looked, there was no one there.

I was seriously paranoid.

Irritated, I hitched my bag higher on my shoulder and continued on.

When I found the building that matched the address I'd been given, I stopped in front of the door and frowned. A chain and deadbolt made it clear the front door was not an option. As I turned away, my gaze caught on a small sign on the front door. *Jughfsld Ruthdkjgh.*

It was written in elvish; an ancient language that had died out a couple hundred years ago. A test.

I brushed my palm over it, using my fae magic to transform the letters into something I could understand.

Visitors use rear entrance.

Booyah.

The alley was empty, and in the silence, I noted how unassuming the place looked from the outside. A nondescript building by the river. No human signs advertising its purpose. No traffic. The SSF was good at blending. Or just vanishing altogether. In fact, they were the best at making things disappear. It would be part of my training; not just defending the planet against evil monsters but making sure no one ever knew they'd been here to begin with.

I thought of my father, out on a gray, rain-soaked night much like this morning—alone. A lump formed in my throat and I resisted the urge to pat my thigh where my contraband was currently secured. Just because I couldn't see a surveillance camera didn't mean I wasn't being watched.

Rounding the back of the building, my boots sloshed through puddles as I made my way to the loading dock entrance. Once there, I hesitated, heart pounding. This was it.

The moment everything changed.

There was no going back. Not to drag racing for cash on the weekends. Not to Lila's Sandwich Shop. Nothing would ever be the same again. Then again, I decided, that was true whether I walked through these doors or not. No matter what, Dad was still gone.

With a wet fist, I banged on the door and stepped back to wait.

A moment later, the door opened.

Large, beady eyes peered out at me from the darkness within.

"Name," said a gruff voice.

The smell of stale breath hit me, right along with a force of power I couldn't quite place in my mental catalog of supes.

"Gem Hawkins, reporting for agent training."

I squinted, trying to get a good look, but his wide, square-cut frame wasn't anything I recognized. Ogre? Giant? According to common belief, both of those had long been extinct. But the smell and size weren't anything I'd ever met before.

"Ugh." He snatched my duffel bag and yanked it open, rummaging through it with fat fingers.

"Excuse me," I said, but he didn't answer.

When he finished, he handed the bag over again.

"What the heck was that for?" I asked.

"Ugh ugh," the beast grunted and promptly slammed the door in my face.

What the hell?

I debated knocking again but then another door opened farther down and a woman stepped out. Her blue glasses and bright red lipstick stood out against the dreary backdrop. She motioned at me to join her.

"Hi, you're Gem?"

I nodded, registering her inner feline as I got close.

"I'm Starla. I'll be escorting you through check-in this morning. This way."

She held the door for me, and I stepped inside, grateful to be out of the rain. The moment the door shut behind me, I shuddered. Goose bumps rose along my arms and neck and dizziness washed over me.

"What the . . ."

I braced a hand on the wall for support.

My awareness of Starla's animal vanished. I could no longer sense her supe signature. Nor could I sense any sort of magic in myself at all.

"Oh, right. Forgive me, I always forget what a shock it is the first few times." I stared at her in confusion. "The training academy is spelled to strip all magics from its recruits."

"Seriously?"

The dizziness began to clear but the sense of wrongness remained.

"Certain training areas allow its use to return to you, but in the dorms and halls and the like, we don't allow it. It's for the safety and protection of all."

I grimaced, not sure I quite agreed with her after seeing the ogre dude at the first door. What if he decided I made a perfect midnight snack?

"Come, let's get you settled and out of those wet clothes."

Starla led the way, and I followed, still a little unsteady

as we navigated the labyrinth of halls. We passed a few closed doors marked as dorms. Finally, Starla led us into an admin area and into a room marked "Medical."

"Go ahead and get out of those clothes and put this on. I'll send the nurse in shortly."

Starla was gone before I could reply.

My clothes weren't a big deal. The cell phone taped to my thigh, however, was. I'd just peeled it off—without yelping at the sting it caused—and stuffed it into the bottom of my duffel when the door opened.

A male fae slipped in and then quickly shut the door again. His brown eyes were wide as he stared back at me, surprise then shock then fear washing over his expression. I was hyper aware of the thin hospital gown I wore, but his eyes never strayed to my body. His panic was evident in the way his pointed ears twitched with each breath.

"Can I help you?" I asked as his gaze darted around the room.

"Listen, if they ask, I was with you last night, okay?"

"Uh—"

Before I could ask exactly what that meant—and what sort of alibi he was hoping for—the door opened again and an older woman in a white lab coat entered. If she was a supe, I had no idea what. My lack of fae senses made it impossible to read her, though if I had to guess, I would have gone with mouse shifter.

"Hello, I'm Leslie, the on-staff nurse here. I'm here to

conduct your entrance exam." Her polite smile faltered when she spotted the male hovering beside me. "Oh, I didn't realize we were doubling up," she said uncertainly.

The male beside me tensed.

I flashed an apologetic smile at Leslie. "I guess Starla didn't realize there was someone in here already."

"Huh. Well, we can't exactly do exams in pairs, can we?"

"Not like I haven't seen it." The male fae spoke up, and when I looked at him in confusion, he winked.

Leslie flushed. "Oh, I see. You two know each other then?"

"Uh, yeah." I caught his side eye and then turned back to her. "We sure do."

My lie was terrible so far.

For good measure, I grabbed his hand in mine and added, "Pretty well, in fact, after last night."

I could hear his sigh and wondered what the hell he'd done last night to so desperately need an alibi today.

"I see." Leslie looked down at a clipboard. "Well, that answers at least two questions on my list." She flipped through papers. "Gem?" She looked up at me for confirmation.

I nodded.

"And you are?" she asked the male.

"Milo," he answered quickly. "Milo Mercer."

She made a few notes and then looked up again.

"Since we're all here, let's go through the Q and A portion, and then I'll split you up for the physical. Gem, how long have you known Milo?"

"Uh, since last night?"

Leslie blinked at me. "I see."

Judgment. So much judgment in her tone. Whatever Milo was running from, it better be good.

"And did either of you have any other . . . partners besides each other in the past ninety days?"

I frowned, thinking of Z. "One."

"I see. And Mr. Mercer?"

"Zero."

Liar.

One look at his guilty expression and I knew he was hiding more than just whatever he needed covered up from last night. Maybe it was my own lack of an interesting social life, but I was intrigued.

"And do either of you have any significant other, er, besides each other, waiting for you when you complete the training program?"

"No," Milo and I said at the same time.

"And do you both understand that when you take the oath to become an agent for the SSF, you renounce all rights to choose a partner or a mate unless approved by the SSF?"

"Whoa, what?" I said at the same time Milo muttered, "Yes."

The nurse arched a brow at me. "You haven't read the handbook?"

"I guess I missed that chapter."

She frowned. "If this isn't something you can swear to, Miss Hawkins, I don't know if the training program is a good fit for you."

Milo squeezed my hand.

"I agree," I said begrudgingly.

Not a big deal. You're not here for a mate, I reminded myself.

But the rules and nosy-ass questions were really starting to piss me off.

After that, the nurse ran through things like medical history and our supe heritage. Milo was full fae while I was half-fae, half-shifter.

"What kind of shifter?" the nurse asked me.

"Griffin."

Her brows rose, but she marked it down. "Don't see many of those anymore. I think the last one we had was . . . ?" Her brow furrowed while she thought.

"Vic Hawkins," I supplied. "My father."

"Oh, my, I didn't realize . . ." Her expression fell. "I was so sorry to hear about his passing. My condolences."

I didn't answer.

Milo squeezed my hand again.

"Well, I think I have everything I need," Leslie said.

"Milo, why don't you wait outside while Gem and I finish up in here."

"Sure." Milo shot me a grateful look. "Thanks," he whispered on his way out.

Leslie ran through a few physical exercises then a few mental ones meant to test whether my fae magic was really stripped. When I couldn't see through a glamour she claimed was really a Jane Washington fantasy novel spelled to look like a bedpan, she seemed satisfied.

When I was given the all clear, Leslie handed me a set of clothes.

I eyed the black leggings and tank as Leslie explained, "Standard issue for all recruits. You'll find six more sets already waiting in your dorm room along with workout gear. The fabric is breathable and allows you to move easily through the rigorous workouts they'll put you through. Starla is outside waiting to escort you to your room."

She opened the door, adding, "Welcome to the SSF. And good luck."

Twenty minutes later, I was standing in a small dorm room, when Milo poked his head inside.

"Hey, thanks again for earlier."

"Do I get to know what I helped cover up?"

He hesitated then shut the door and lowered his voice. "His name is Miguel. He bartends in the Quarter and is here illegally."

"So, are you worried about admitting you're gay or that your boyfriend is undocumented?"

"Yes."

My heart hurt for the fear in his eyes. "Milo, the SSF has been accepting of sexual orientation long before humans finally started to come around. They don't care."

"Most of them don't," he agreed. "But I'm not sure that's true for Rodrigo Garcia. Word is, he's a homophobic perv who likes to hit on the female recruits by day and the male recruits by night. I'm not looking to get on his radar, if you know what I mean."

"I read about him," I said darkly. "And if he so much as side eyes either of us, I'll stab him with a rusty fork."

Milo lifted a brow. "And get kicked out on your ass for doing it."

"Point taken. I'm sorry you have to lie about being gay."

Milo hesitated. "That's not exactly the only reason. What if I told you Miguel's legal status wasn't a human problem."

My eyes widened. "Milo, you slept with a freaking demon?"

He winced. "He's only a quarter demon. It's not like he's got four heads or something. Geez. Although . . ." His eyes lit up. "What if he had four dicks? That would be awesome."

I shook my head.

Milo tensed. "You're not going to rat on me, are you?"

"Of course not. I'm the last one to judge."

He smirked. "Is that because you lied?"

"I don't care who they think I slept with, although those questions were nosy as hell."

"I'm not talking about being my faux fornicator. You're not just a griffin shifter, Gem Hawkins."

I went still.

How the hell did he know? With my magic gone, I couldn't sense a rata demon from a cat right now.

"Relax. Your secret's safe. And now we're even."

"You can sense my magic?" I asked.

"I can sense a liar," he corrected. "A gift that apparently goes beyond magic ability. I got it from my momma, and she can sense a liar from three dimensions away."

I slumped onto the tiny twin mattress. "Or maybe I just suck at it."

He laughed.

Through the speaker overhead, a voice sounded. "All recruits, report to the auditorium for orientation."

Milo and I shared a look.

"Guess that's us," I said.

He held out his hand, wiggling his brows. "Ready, lover?"

I let him pull me to my feet, and we started for the door. "I guess we'll find out."

SIX

Milo and I followed the other recruits winding their way through the halls and up the stairs. We ended up in a large auditorium with stadium seating.

"Turnout's impressive," Milo said as we passed through the open doors.

I barely had a chance to murmur an agreement when a pop rang in my ears and an electric shock shuddered through me.

My skin buzzed as my magic returned.

Milo and I exchanged a look.

"That was trippy," he said.

"Is this going to be an everyday thing?"

"You get used to it," said another voice.

I looked over at the woman who'd spoken. Her name tag read Professor Landis.

"It feels like I'm being stripped naked and then redressing in front of everyone," I told her.

She laughed. "Yeah, I guess it's easier to adjust if you don't mind being naked in front of strangers."

Milo beamed. "Guess I've got a leg up then."

Gran would love him.

I exhaled, relieved at the sensation of feeling whole again, and followed him up the aisle.

By the time we found seats, the space was nearly full. I scanned the faces filling the seats, surprised at how many there were. The building was a lot larger on the inside than it had looked from the outside.

"Half these guys won't make it," I said.

"As long as that half doesn't include us," Milo said.

Starla, the woman who'd greeted me earlier, stepped up to the center arena. "Attention, please."

Her voice filled the room as easily as if she'd had a microphone.

The rest of the recruits quieted.

"Welcome to the Supernatural Security Force Training Facility for New Orleans," she announced.

A large portion of the recruits cheered.

Starla flashed her white teeth then motioned for everyone to quiet again.

"My name is Starla Hoffman, and I'm the training coordinator among other things here at the SSFTF."

"Angel balls, that acronym is a mouthful," Milo muttered.

A male recruit in a stiff-collared shirt gave Milo a dirty look. His warlock energy sputtered around his aura in a not-so-promising display. "Watch your mouth," he said haughtily before promptly ignoring us.

Milo rolled his eyes.

"For the next few months," Starla continued, "you will be instructed and evaluated in all the ways we can possibly prepare you for demon hunting. That is, of course, the reason you're here, and while a number of you will earn that title and go on to the prestigious position of detective, many will not.

"Those that don't show an aptitude for the hunt can still earn an important place among the SSF's finest. Administrative positions are just as vital to what we do here. Not to mention trainers, portal monitors, and a host of other crucial positions."

"Portal monitor?" Milo whispered. "Why don't they just call it what it is: babysitter."

I snorted.

A brunette in the row ahead of us cleared her throat pointedly.

When Milo winked at her, she glared at him then me.

Starla continued, "Please keep in mind, our trainers are the best there is when it comes to placement. If you fail to display an aptitude or skill set for any of the positions the SSF is currently looking to fill, you may be dismissed. The SSF only takes the best of the best, and we sincerely hope you use this knowledge to dedicate yourself to success while you're here at the SSFTF, or the 'Tiff' as we affectionately call it."

"The Tiff?" Milo repeated. "Dude. Lame. I could think of such better ideas for—"

"Don't you have any respect?" The brunette in front of us scrunched up her face as she stared accusingly back at Milo and me. Pale skin. Red eyes. I was too surprised by the fact that she was a vamp to even reply to her.

"Respect, yes. Filter, not so much," Milo admitted.

"Ugh." The girl turned away. "Blue collar supes are so annoying."

Blue collar? Really? Coming from a vamp, I couldn't help but laugh. Vamps had once been considered a superior race. Until the Nephilim had deemed them demon-spawn and nearly hunted them all to extinction. Now, the label had been lifted but the prejudice had not. Vamps these days were rare. A stuck-up vamp even rarer.

She had balls to talk down to us, I'd give her that.

"There are a few rules to note during your time as a recruit," Starla went on, an edge creeping into her voice. "First, there will be no intermingling with the other recruits beyond mentorship, sparring partners, and necessary tutoring. Any fraternization outside platonic interaction is grounds for immediate dismissal. Second, all magic will be stripped except as provided for necessary combat and skill development while under the guidance of your instructors. Any unauthorized magic use is grounds for expulsion."

Milo whistled low.

"Strict rules," I said in a low voice.

"Looks like our lover's tryst will have to end here." Milo grinned.

The brunette turned her head just enough that I caught her expression. Her pale face flushed, and she looked sufficiently scandalized.

I choked back a laugh.

"Lastly, for the duration of your training, you will remain here at the Tiff. There will be authorized field trips to test your development as you near the end of your training, but these are the only sanctioned leave times. Otherwise, you are a resident of the Tiff and all cell phone use, television, radio, mobile phones, or any other contact with the outside world is prohibited. We ask that you give us your full concentration and attention until we've shaped you into one of our best."

I'd already known this last part, but it still grated that I wouldn't be able to check in with my mother until I was finished here.

Starla continued with a warning about how important it was to be on time. "Thank you all for your commitment to the safety of the supernatural community," she said. "On behalf of the SSF, welcome and good luck."

On the heel of her words, schedules were conjured, appearing in each of our laps on a soft puff of air.

I grabbed mine and scanned the list of classes then compared it to Milo's.

A hum of voices rose as the other recruits chatted with their neighbors about shared classes.

"PT at seven a.m.? Are they insane?" I demanded.

"What's PT?" Milo frowned.

"Physical Training," I said. When his expression remained blank, I added, "Exercise?"

"Cool, I've been meaning to get into shape."

"You didn't do anything before coming here?" I asked.

"I thought that's what the academy was for."

I stared at him. "I ran two miles a day for the last six weeks just to prepare."

"I went clubbing Friday *and* Saturday for the last six weeks. Also to prepare. You think all that dancing counts?"

"I'm going to venture a guess and say no."

"I'll be fine," he said, waving away my concern. "My libido's good for distance."

I raised a brow. "You know libido and endurance aren't the same thing, right?"

He winked. "Aren't they, though? Besides, my PT is in the afternoon. I've got plenty of time to carb up. What else you got?"

"We have History and Demon Tracking together," I said.

"Ugh. Demon Tracking with Rodrigo Garcia," Milo added, pointing to the name on the schedule.

"At least we can have each other's backs."

"The two amigos," Milo said.

"Want a third amigo?"

I looked up at the male standing on my left. He'd been sitting a few seats away, but now closed the distance with a friendly smile. Dark eyes peered out from behind shaggy hair. He was younger than me by a couple of years, but his arms and chest were bulky with muscle. With my magic back, my fae senses pegged him for a shifter.

Milo perked up, gesturing to the empty chair beside me. "Have a seat, friend."

"I'm Tony." The male held out his hand, and Milo took it eagerly.

"Milo."

"Gem," I said, shaking my head at Milo's sexual energy already building.

My fae senses were great at detecting everything from glamours to strange smells, and that included pheromones —especially those of my own kind. If Milo and I were going to be friends, I needed to start sitting downwind in social situations.

"You guys into this whole secret code name Tiff nonsense?" Tony's brows rose, and the brunette from earlier turned to side-eye him before going back to her own conversation.

"Not nearly as much as that chick is," Milo said, and Tony grinned.

"*That chick's* name is Faith," she snapped. "And you three are beyond rude."

My brows lifted as she flipped her hair and motioned to her friends. They all got up and left without another word.

Milo whistled.

"She won't even need a weapon issued," he said. "She can just use that stick up her ass."

Tony snorted.

From across the room, I caught Starla watching us. Unease rippled through me and I had the distinct impression she'd heard us despite the distance and the fact that she was locked in conversation with the professor who'd spoken to us on the way in.

Finally, she looked away, and I turned back to Tony.

"Werewolf?" I asked, noting the shifter scent he gave off.

Tony nodded. "Fae?" he asked, gesturing between us, his gaze darting to each of our pointed ears.

"Guilty," Milo said.

"Half," I said.

"Cool." Tony didn't ask what my other half was, and I decided right there he was someone I could hang with.

"Hey, you're fae, right?"

I looked up at a slender girl with dirty blonde hair, and my eyes went wide.

She was soaked. And not just wet but . . . overflowing. Water pooled then ran from the top of her head—which was also draped in what looked like lily pads. The water ran in sheets down the rest of her, soaking the seaweed hanging off her clothes. What the hell?

"Uh, yeah," I said warily.

"Does that mean you have the power to undo a spell?"

"Depends on the spell," I said.

"What happened?" Milo asked.

She hesitated then dropped into the empty chair on Milo's other side. A squish sounded and water began to pool on the chair around her. A steady drip began to puddle on the floor underneath where she sat.

"I think my mom was trying to help make sure I didn't get distracted by fraternization," she said with a grimace.

"So she turned you into a koi pond?" Milo asked.

"Basically," the girl said.

I watched as her hair parted and seaweed began to grow out of her scalp at an alarming rate. More water poured from her forehead onto her shoulders and already soaked clothes.

"Girlfriend, your momma has serious issues with over-protectiveness," Milo said.

"I know. It wasn't a problem in the dorms where our magic was stripped but now . . ."

"Now you need some drying out," I finished.

She nodded.

Milo and I leaned in and together, placed a hand on her arm. Immediately, the warmth of magic rushed through my hand and into her wet skin. My fae senses easily grabbed ahold of the glamour spell that had been cast and shattered it. The water stopped leaking from her head. Seaweed dried out and fell away as the glamour dissolved.

When we sat back, the girl smiled and wrung out her clothes.

"Sorry, you'll have to change if you want to get completely dry," I told her.

"No, you've done more than enough. Thank you," she said. "I'm Fiona."

She held out her hand, and we all shook, offering quick introductions.

When she got to Tony, his eyes lit up with an interested gleam, and he held onto her slender hand longer than necessary.

"Witch?" I asked her.

She nodded. "Not very useful against demon fighting but I plan to study extra hard with weapons to make up for it."

Her determination was admirable, if not a little worrisome. She was tiny as hell with no muscle build and a jumpiness to her that had me wondering just how effective she'd be against a six-foot demon from Hell. But she was here, which meant the SSF recruiters had seen something promising.

"What's your schedule?" I asked.

She handed it over, the ink a little runny from where it had gotten wet, and we all compared.

"Looks like we have Protocol and Policies together," Tony said, his excitement obvious.

But Fiona was looking at Milo. "What about you?" she asked.

"Nothing in common," he said with a shrug. "But there's always meal times."

She nodded. "I heard one of the other recruits talking about how the kitchen is spelled to offer our preferred foods based on our species. It's kind of amazing how they can accommodate so many different supes at once."

"Amazing," Tony agreed, his entire attention focused on Fiona.

I groaned inwardly. As a fae, that meant nothing but greens. My shapeshifter side was a little more carnivorous than that—not that I could chance telling the staff that.

Milo stood and offered his hand to Fiona. "Come on, my little wet noodle, let's get you back to your room so you can dry off before lights out."

"Thanks, I'm exhausted," she admitted.

"Lead the way."

Tony and I fell into step behind them, and we made our way out. The magic sizzled then slid away as we passed through the doors that led back to our dorm rooms. I tried not to notice the hollow ache in my chest it left behind.

Tony grimaced. "I don't know that I'll ever get used to that feeling."

"Tell me about it," Milo said. "The only stripping I want to do is these clothes from my skin."

He winked, and the others laughed. I groaned, glad I couldn't pick up on all the pheromone scents that would follow a comment like that.

SEVEN

Milo was waiting for me when I emerged from my room the next morning. PT had been as bad as expected. Maybe worse. We'd started with a two-mile run for warm-up with promises for three miles tomorrow. Then, it had been weight lifting and resistance training for another hour on top of that. I was already exhausted, and I hadn't even made it to breakfast yet. Even the hot shower afterward hadn't done much to soothe my already-sore body.

"Whoa, you look like—"

"I need coffee."

"Exactly what I was going to say."

I shot him a look as we fell into step.

"Is this going to be a thing?" I asked as we made our way to the dining hall.

"Is what going to be a thing?"

"You waiting for me, walking with me. Are we friends?"

"I mean, nurse Leslie thinks we slept together. I think the logical thing is to try out friendship, don't you think?"

Rather than try to answer a statement like that, I walked faster, beelining for the coffee station on the far wall of the dining area. Milo followed.

"If you don't want to be friends, we can be frenemies," he said.

"What's a frenemy?"

He stopped and gawked at me. "Haven't you ever seen *Mean Girls*?"

"What's that? Like a web show or something?"

"Dear Baby Jesus. It's a cult classic. How do you not know—"

I sighed. "Okay, we can be friends if you promise not to make me watch whatever thing you're judging me for not watching."

His brows dipped in what was obviously more judgment.

I poured a cup of coffee and then mixed in more creamer than any one creature probably needed.

"Do we have a deal?" I asked, turning back to find Milo sizing me up.

"Fine, but if I tell you to wear pink on Wednesday, you have to do it, no questions asked."

"Why would I do that?"

"Because we're friends," he said as if that was the only answer I should need.

"Fine. But I look better in magenta."

His grin was slow and wide. "The fact that you just said 'magenta' erases my doubts. Come on, lover, we're going to be late."

I wasn't sure whether to be relieved or worried that Milo was in my first class. He was obviously a morning person and maybe even a demon-spawn considering his level of cheer and lack of caffeine.

I gulped down my coffee and wished I'd thought to double fist it. Before I could sneak back for a refill, an older man in a Hawaiian print button-down walked in, closing the door behind him.

"Welcome to History and Heritage. For the next few weeks, we're going to be talking about the formation of the SSF. How we got our start and what our role is as it relates to demons, Nephilim, and the world around us. I'm Professor Wayne, and I've been with the agency for sixteen years. In fact, I started as an analyst for the portal division and worked my way up and over from there. Can anyone tell me what that department does?"

A male recruit raised his hand. I recognized him as the warlock who'd fussed at Milo yesterday during orientation. He was probably not very powerful judging by the ink stains on his fingers. Only lower level magicians still wrote out their spells. Everyone else was digital these days. Or oral.

"The portal division is in charge of managing the active portals in its district," the warlock said in a nasally voice. "Analysts provide data on what kinds of demons have come through and how long since the portal was last used. They pinpoint where a demon entered the city and how long it's been loose."

"Good. What's your name, kid?"

"Langdon Potts."

"Keep it up, Potts."

The warlock looked sufficiently pleased with himself. Total nerd, I decided, and possible tutor if I ended up needing the help. School had never been my strong suit. But then I'd never needed to graduate in order to avenge a murder either.

"And who can tell me when the first demon appeared in the world?"

"Exactly one hundred years ago in June," said a female voice. "This summer solstice marks the centennial."

I didn't even have to turn to know which recruit had spoken. The brunette from yesterday's assembly sat two rows over in the front. Her folded hands and fresh notebook screamed "teacher's pet." After the interaction we'd had during orientation, I wasn't surprised.

Professor Wayne flashed her a smile. "Correct, Miss. . .?"

"Faith Burkhart."

"Burkhart." Professor Wayne tapped his chin. "I know that name. Your mother is a scientist?"

"Geneticist," Faith said, tossing her chestnut hair as she spoke.

"Ah. Yes. Brilliant mind. I've read her research on using RNA splicing on supes to cure human diseases. Very intriguing."

Faith preened. "She's my mentor and biggest cheerleader."

Suddenly, the "blue collar" comment made sense.

Out of the corner of my eye, I caught Milo pretending to stick his finger down his throat in a gagging motion.

"Now, who can tell me when the first Nephilim appeared?"

Milo muttered, "When someone stared into a broken mirror and said Bloody Mary three times in the dark."

I choked on a laugh as the rest of the class erupted. Faith shot Milo a dirty look. Professor Wayne seemed torn between amusement and reproach.

"What's your name, kid?" he asked.

"Milo Greene."

"Tell you what, Milo. You answer my other questions correctly and I'll overlook the comedic commentary."

"Forever?" Milo quipped.

"Depends on how many correct answers you can give me."

Milo smirked. "The Neph showed up within days of the first wave of demons. Convenient but apparently not a setup as time works differently in the big chill-out in the sky. According to the stories passed down by the Head Nephs, the demon war started in the Underworld, spilled into the Overworld, then ended up here, in the in-between. We've been trying to plug the holes ever since."

Silence followed.

"Well." Professor Wayne cleared his throat. "That's the most succinct and possibly entertaining way I've heard it explained."

"And the most ignorant," Faith muttered.

Milo flipped her off, and her eyes widened in indignation. She opened her mouth to respond.

"What about the SSF?" Professor Wayne asked before Faith could get a word out. "Who wants to give the backstory of the organization you now work for?" His eyes swept the room and landed on me. "Miss...?"

"Gem Hawkins," I said, knowing full well what would follow.

As expected, his eyes lit up with recognition. "Any relation to Vic Hawkins?"

"I'm his daughter."

Faith's eyes narrowed.

"A legacy, eh? In that case, I'm interested to hear your answer."

"The SSF was founded after the first level four demon was recorded," I said.

"Location of the four?" the professor challenged.

"Right here in the French Quarter," I said.

He nodded. "Go on."

"The Nephilim realized they needed help—"

"Wanted help," Faith corrected. I shot her a look, and she added, "The Nephilim don't *need* us. They're stronger and more powerful than any supe will ever be." She batted her lashes at the professor. "We are honored to serve alongside them in keeping the world safe from evil."

"And who will save us from you?"

The words slipped out before I could stop them.

Faith gave me a look that could have given demon-poison a run for its money.

Professor Wayne just laughed.

"I see a rivalry has already formed. All in good fun, of course."

"Of course," I reassured him.

Faith didn't answer, and I knew I'd just made myself her number one target. Something about her syrupy-sweet smile told me I would have been better off facing down a level four hellhound than Faith Burkhart.

"*That's* a frenemy," Milo whispered, and I shot him a look.

"You were saying, Miss Hawkins?"

I looked back at Professor Wayne. "A year after the

SSF was founded, the Nephilim formed the council, which oversees all of the major decisions of the organization and all of its employees. For the first sixty-five years, the council consisted of only Nephilim. Ten years ago, they opened a seat to the supes by way of general election."

"And who sits on the board for the supes now?" Professor Wayne prompted.

"No one," I answered, anger tightening my chest. "Four years ago, John Fulburn, the supe council member was assassinated, and the Nephilim declared it too dangerous to allow another to sit in his place. The seat has remained empty ever since."

"I heard the seat was eliminated last year," someone else put in.

"For our safety," Faith said.

"I heard it was budget cuts," said another recruit.

"Try elitism," I said, and Professor Wayne lifted a brow.

"Interesting theory, Miss Hawkins. I look forward to reading your thoughts on the reorganization of the International Coalition and how it affects our own city's rate of recruitment." He turned to the rest of the room. "You'll all write a two-thousand word essay on the subject. Due tomorrow."

The others groaned.

I studied the professor, trying to decide if he'd assigned the paper based on my comments or if he'd intended it all along. Before I could form a theory, he glanced at Faith then back to me.

"We'll use the essay as a basis for a class debate. Faith, why don't you captain one team and Gem can captain the other."

I cringed at the idea of pitting myself against Faith. Regardless of my personal feelings, I didn't want any more enemies if I could help it.

"Sir, I'd rather—"

"I look forward to it," Faith said with a wild gleam lighting her red eyes.

Of course she did.

A viper always looked forward to a chance to spew its venom.

THERE WERE zero familiar faces in my next class, and after what had happened in History, I was relieved to be just another face in the crowd. The training room had been cleared of any desks or seating and was nothing more than mats from wall to wall with a large selection of various handheld weapons displayed near the doors.

I found a spot on the mat and sat like the other recruits.

"Hey, I'm Leedle."

A female recruits on my right stuck her hand out.

I shook it, noting the glittery dust to her cheeks that almost resembled freckles and the wings folded against the inside of her racerback tank. Pixie then.

"Gem," I said.

"Love the hair." She flashed a quick smile, and I realized our short blonde cuts were nearly identical.

"Good morning and welcome to Weapons 101."

I had to crane my neck to see the female instructor who spoke from the front of the room. Even with the rest of the recruits sitting, she was barely visible over their heads.

Dressed in full black, the leather of her pants crinkled as she paced back and forth. Her hands were clasped behind her back and her hair was pulled up in a high ponytail. Her looks were practical—and badass. And it made me wonder if I wasn't underestimating her. Any woman, regardless of how short or small, who was given a job as weapons instructor probably knew her shit.

"I'm Professor Kinrade, and I'll be your instructor for all things weapon-related."

One of the recruits snorted and Professor Kinrade stopped short to glare at him.

"Name?" she demanded.

"Charles Lane."

"Supe category?"

"Boar shifter."

Beside me, Leedle muttered, "Explains some things."

"Do you have an opinion about my ability to instruct this class, Charles Lane?"

"You don't look like much of a threat," he said, and I shook my head.

One look at Professor Kinrade's gleaming expression and I knew he was going to live to regret that statement.

"Come on up. You can be my first volunteer."

Charles sauntered to the front, and Professor Kinrade resumed her talk.

"Today, we'll go over each weapon and you'll have a chance to play with them, feel their weight, and get comfortable with the proper hold for each one. Starting tomorrow, you'll need a partner for sparring. We use live weapons, people, so stay alert. If you get too distracted, you just might end up dead, and I don't want to do that kind of paperwork, are we clear?"

Leedle and I exchanged a wary look.

"Good." The professor strode to the weapons display and pulled down a short-handled blade.

"Charles, want to tell me what this is?"

"A knife."

A few recruits snickered.

Kinrade wasn't amused.

"An astute observation. Do you know what kind?"

Charles looked away, still doing his best to seem confident. "The sharp kind?"

Kinrade turned to the rest of us. "This is a Kershaw. It's the easiest weapon to conceal carry in terms of weight and placement. It's also the most accurate for long distance throwing and the most lethal in close combat. It's an agency favorite, which means you'll all be issued one of these along with a couple of other staples. Charles?"

She held out the knife.

He took it awkwardly.

"Now, attack," she said.

His brows lifted. "You want me to knife you?"

Her smirk was lethal. "I want you to try."

Charles hesitated another moment then shrugged in acceptance. When he lunged, Kinrade danced away easily. Her movements were faster than I'd ever seen especially without magic, but in less than a blink, she'd dodged him and doubled back to wrap her arm around his throat.

Charles gagged. His face reddened, and I knew she'd squeezed tight enough to cut off his oxygen.

"Your most important lesson is this," she said calmly. "Being armed doesn't make you more dangerous than they are. Know how to use that weapon skillfully or don't use it all. At the end of the day, you have to be faster and you have to know how to fight with your own two hands."

Charles began choking, and she promptly released him. He gasped, bending at the waist as he sucked in air.

Kinrade grabbed the knife from his limp hand and returned it to the wall.

"Sit down, Lane," she said.

Charles dropped to the mat, looking relieved.

The rest of class was a piece by piece instructional on the various weapons we'd be training with. At the end, Kinrade assigned partners, and I ended up paired with Leedle.

"Looks like we're going to have to kick each other's asses starting tomorrow," she said as class broke up.

I eyed her wings, knowing I'd have to work extra hard to keep up with her in a fight.

"Relax," she said sadly. "They won't work until the wards are lifted."

"Seriously?"

"Apparently the wards strip everything, so now I've got a pair of shower curtains hanging down my back."

"Let me know if you need help reaching them in the shower," one of the male recruits called over.

"Fulton, if my wings were melting off my body, I wouldn't call you," she said.

"Ouch," said the guy beside him.

Fulton just smirked and disappeared into the crowd headed for the dining hall.

"Hawkins."

I turned back and saw Kinrade watching me from doorway.

"I'll catch up with you later," Leedle said with a wave.

"See you." I doubled back to the training room. "Ma'am."

"You're a Hawkins. As in, Vic Hawkins' daughter."

"Yes, ma'am." My stomach sank. Of course she'd called me back to discuss my legacy status.

"I'd like to establish here and now that doesn't mean an easy ride for you, no matter how good of an agent your father was."

"Of course. I wouldn't expect."

She thrust a book at me hard enough to elicit a grunt.

I frowned down at the thick volume and read the title: Myth & Modern Century Supes.

"What's this?" I asked.

"Let's call it extra credit."

"Why do I need extra—?"

"Class ended, Miss Hawkins. That means all of your questions will have to hold until tomorrow."

I opened my mouth to argue but was cut off with the door clicking shut in my face.

So this was what it meant to be a legacy.

On a sigh, I hurried to drop the book at my dorm room before lunch. This thing was ridiculously heavy, and I didn't want to lug it around on top of everything else my afternoon instructors might give us.

The dorm halls were empty, and without the crowd of other recruits pushing against me, I found my room again easily enough. Pressing my finger to the electronic reader, I listened for the click of the lock and then pushed the door open.

Inside, I stopped and surveyed the room.

Nothing had moved but there was an envelope on my unmade bed that hadn't been there before.

My breath turned shallow, and my senses went on high alert.

Without my fae hearing or sense of smell, it was impossible to identify who might have put it there.

With slow, measured movements, I crossed the room and checked the tiny closet.

Empty.

None of my clothes were missing.

Doubling back, I checked under the mattress and found my hidden cell still tucked where I'd left it.

With relief, I peered down at the envelope.

There was no name written on the front. And without magic, no signature detectable from the creature who'd left it.

I picked it up and sniffed anyway.

Nothing.

Stupid mundane senses.

With careful fingers, I peeled back the flap and pulled out the single sheet of paper inside.

You shouldn't have come.

The words were handwritten and messy enough to be almost unreadable.

I frowned, turning the paper over in my hands, but there was nothing else to indicate who might have sent this.

My thoughts drifted to the stranger in the alley. The one who'd threatened me away from the academy. But without the proper credentials, there was no way he'd have access to the Tiff. Then again, if my suspicions were right, whoever was behind that message probably had the title and the position to get in here.

On the other hand, it could have been any one of the students here at the Tiff. Faith came to mind, but I immediately dismissed the idea. I had a feeling her penmanship was better than this. And she wouldn't stoop to vague notes. She'd tell me to my face.

One of the instructors, maybe?

It was a possibility, especially after the way they all seemed to sour toward me once they found out I was a legacy.

Hell, at this point, the list of who wouldn't write this was shorter than the list of who would.

Frustrated, I shoved the paper back into the envelope and slid the whole thing into my desk drawer. After I'd stashed the textbook Kinrade had given me, I headed for the door, stomach growling. If I missed lunch, whoever wrote that note was going to wish they hadn't made me hangry.

Just before the dining hall, I spotted Starla coming toward me.

"Gem. There you are. I was beginning to worry."

"I had to put away a textbook."

"Would you mind taking a walk with me?"

"Sure. Everything okay?"

"Everything's great."

She ushered me aside so a couple of recruits could pass us. She lowered her voice and said, "There was a small hiccup at the main entrance of the Tiff just now, and I wanted to check in with you about it."

"What kind of hiccup?" I asked, inching even farther from listening ears.

"That depends. Are you acquainted with a warlock who called himself Z?"

For once, I was glad for the magic stripping that meant supes couldn't hear us from miles off.

"I'm . . . acquainted, yes."

"I see. Well, apparently he was worried when you didn't return his phone calls. He used a locator spell to track you here and was found trying to spell his way past security."

My jaw dropped.

"That twatwaffle."

Starla blinked. "Is that your official response?"

"My . . . No. Sorry." Clearly, I'd been hanging with Gran too long. "Look, I spoke with Z before reporting in and made it clear he wouldn't be hearing from me for a while."

"And did you tell him where you'd be?"

"No way. I didn't have a location to give him anyway."

"Does he know you work for the SSF?"

"No," I said firmly. "Hell, he probably wouldn't believe me if I'd told him."

"I see. That's all I needed to know."

She moved to step around me.

"Wait. Is he in trouble?"

She tilted her head. "Do you want him to be?"

I frowned, trying to decide. "He's an idiot, but he's not a criminal," I said finally.

She nodded. "I'll take care of it."

She strode off with a purposeful march, leaving me to wonder what exactly would become of my ex. And whether I'd become an accessory if I ever asked.

EIGHT

Lunch was surprisingly good. I inhaled a quinoa salad and two pieces of chocolate cake that made me moan out loud until several of the other recruits began to stare. I caught a red-headed male watching me and paused, my fork hallway to my mouth. He winked at the same time Milo elbowed me.

"You might want to save your performance for a more private audience, superstar."

"It's so damn good," I said around a mouthful of baked sugary goodness.

Milo chuckled. "That's what she said."

Tony snickered, and Fiona flushed.

"No sex talk while I'm eating chocolate," I said.

"Why does that matter?" Tony asked.

"It feels like cheating," I told him as I polished off the last of it.

Fiona giggled.

I turned to the buffet line, eyeing the choices and debating on seconds.

"If you're still hungry, you can have the rest of my Rueben," Fiona offered, holding it out.

I shuddered.

"No thanks. I don't eat anything held together by bread."

"Why not?" Tony asked.

"Long story," I grumbled.

"Well, I don't discriminate," Tony said, taking the sandwich for himself.

"You're like a vacuum," Milo told him as he practically inhaled what was left.

"State Fair hot dog eating champ four years in a row," Tony said, his voice muffled around the food.

"Ohh, we have a champion in our mix," I said with a laugh.

"Two." Milo nudged my shoulder.

I shot him a look.

"Gem is the reigning queen of the strip down at the docks."

Tony eyed me with new interest—and respect. "You drive?"

"Drive?" Fiona repeated, clearly confused.

"Drag racing," Tony explained.

"Oh." Her eyes lit. "Wow. Congrats."

I scowled at them all. "Lower your voices. You want it getting around I'm part of an illegal racing club?"

I shot a look toward the dining hall doors but none of the professors were in sight. Other than kitchen staff restocking the buffets, we were pretty much left alone.

"What club?" Tony asked in a low voice.

I bit my lip. "Clutch."

Tony's eyes widened. "Clutch is the number one racing club in the state. What's your handle?"

"Hawk."

Tony whistled. "No shit. I've heard of you."

"Told you our girl is famous," Milo said.

"How do you even know about that?" I asked.

He tapped his temple. "It's a gift."

I shook my head. "Well, keep your gift quiet around here. The Tiff doesn't know about my past career, and I'd like to keep it that way."

Milo muttered something about secrets being a pain in the ass, and we all went back to eating.

After lunch, Tony headed off to History and Heritage while Milo, Fiona, and I made our way to Demon Tracking. The zip of my magic returning hit me unexpectedly as I walked in.

I sucked in a sharp breath as the buzz of my own power rippled through me.

"There's only one feeling better, am I right?"

I looked over and frowned at the man who'd spoken.

He wore a collared shirt with the SSF logo emblazoned on the lapel, and that alone had me biting my tongue to keep from snapping a comeback. He smirked, as if he knew he'd just baited me into a losing battle.

With a raking gaze, he scanned the length of me. A second later, coyote pheromones hit me hard enough to make my eyes water. Then his gaze shifted to Fiona, and the scent only intensified.

I grabbed Milo's arm for support and let him lead me to a seat. Fiona trailed behind, and I grabbed her sleeve, pulling her toward the seat between us.

"What are you—?" she began.

"Just sit. Don't make eye contact and don't raise your hand," I told her.

She nodded and ducked her head, no questions asked.

Over her head, Milo waved a hand in front of his nose. I couldn't blame him. If the smell was any indication, everything I'd heard about Rodrigo Garcia was true.

"Good afternoon, recruits. I'm Professor Garcia." The professor's eyes landed on a female in the front row. "You can call me Rodrigo. Or just Rigo, if you prefer. In this class, you'll learn everything you need to know about tracking and killing demons."

Someone slid into the chair next to mine.

"Hey," a voice whispered.

I looked over at the redheaded male from lunch. His features were handsome, and his smile was friendly.

"Hey."

More importantly, he didn't automatically start trying to mind-screw me. His fox shifter scent was a welcome distraction from Rigo's stench. I leaned in closer to inhale more of it. Anything to overpower that.

"I'm Cliff."

"Gem."

"Did I miss anything?" he asked.

I shook my head. "No, we—"

Something hard rapped against my desk.

I jumped and looked up at Rigo standing over us, some sort of wooden baton clutched in his thick hand. One end had been whittled down to a sharpened point. The blunt end rested on my desk.

"This guy bothering you?" Rigo asked me.

"No."

Rigo stared at Cliff. "See that you mind yourself around the females," he said finally. "Would hate to see you dismissed because you couldn't keep it in your pants."

I blinked.

Rigo shot me a smile, and my stomach churned.

"Sir, I was just—" Cliff began.

"Put a sock in it, recruit. We've got demons to kill."

Rigo walked to the front of the room and caught the eye of

a witch in the front row. "Lots of adrenaline and hormones to deal with in the field."

He winked.

She frowned.

I bit my tongue.

It was going to be a long three months.

THE FIRST WEEK of training passed in a blur of physical exhaustion. Between the grueling demands of my workouts and the late-night reading I did to keep up with the written work, I was a walking zombie. Magic helped to wake me up, but that only happened during the demon-hunting sessions inside the arena. Everywhere else, magic was stripped, and I was forced to admit how much I'd relied on my fae gifts in the past.

Fiona, Tony, and Milo quickly became my tribe despite my promise to myself about not getting too close to anyone. It didn't take long for Milo's jokes, Fiona's sweetness, and Tony's laid-back attitude to become something I depended on to get through the rest of it.

Not all of the students were here to socialize and not

all of them were thrilled about competing against a legacy. I kept my head down and my homework done, and after a few days, the worst of the comments tapered off. I suspected everyone was too damn tired to keep up their bullying.

Seven days a week, we did cardio. Four of the seven also included strength and resistance training. No magic. No supe skills to help us power through.

By the end of the following Monday, every one of our foursome was bleary-eyed and quiet over dinner. The rest of the dining hall was similarly subdued.

When I'd nearly finished my food, Fiona and Tony made an excuse about a study date and slipped away together.

"So much for that idea," Milo muttered, watching them go.

I didn't ask what he meant by it. I'd already seen enough of his longing glances aimed at Tony to know. I'd also seen Fiona's stolen looks become aimed less at Milo and more at Tony. But I hadn't mentioned that to either of them.

After hearing about Z's desperate attempt to breach the Tiff last week, I was feeling pretty done with all relationships—and that included playing matchmaker with my friends.

"Plenty of other fish," I told him instead, but he didn't answer.

"Hey, Gem."

I looked up at the fox shifter from my demon-hunting class.

"Hey," I said. "Cliff, right?"

"Yeah." He flashed a tentative smile. I decided he was cute in a boyish sort of way. Not enough to make me rethink my current vow of celibacy though. "Listen, a few of us are headed up to the hot tub after dinner to soak off some of the soreness. Want to come?"

"There's a hot tub?" Milo demanded, dropping his fork onto his tray. "Why am I just now hearing about this?"

"It's only accessible to senior recruits." Cliff leaned forward and lowered his voice. "My roomie gave me the code before he tested out last week."

I hesitated. I already had a few instructors riding my ass for being a legacy. Trouble wasn't something I could afford, and I had miles to go before I'd be considered a senior recruit.

"Sounds like a party," Milo said, smiling up at Cliff a little dreamily.

We really needed to talk about his flirting issues.

"Great. See you at eight," Cliff said, still looking at me as he strode away.

"Score," Milo said when he was gone. "We get a soak and a chance to befriend some new eye candy."

"You'll have to let me know how it goes."

I rose, tray in hand, and headed for the trash.

"Whoa." Milo jumped up and followed me. "What do you mean? You're not coming with?"

"Can't." I dumped my tray and started for the exit. "I have a mountain of reading to do before tomorrow's evidence procedures lecture."

Milo tossed his entire tray into the trash and hurried to catch up. I decided not to point out he was supposed to return the tray itself.

"Uh, *uno problemo*, lover. Cliff was inviting *you*. I'm clearly your plus one here. Which means without you, I'm minus two."

I shot him a look. "That doesn't even make mathematical sense."

"Well, whose fault is that?" he asked haughtily.

I groaned.

"Come on, Gem. I need cheering up," he said, pouting. "Tony is into Fiona, and I'm lonely, so lonely—"

He started singing the words, and I caved. "Fine." I held up a hand. "I'll go."

"Really?" The pouting evaporated, replaced by excitement.

I'd been totally played.

"For one hour. That'll get you in, as you say, and after that, you do what you want."

"Deal." He beamed at me then flounced down the hall toward his room. "I need to go pick out which swimsuit I'm wearing. See you soon."

I shook my head and returned to my room, already regretting my decision.

At seven fifty, I was halfway into my suit when someone knocked. Milo poked his head in without waiting, and I scowled at him as I pulled the straps up over my shoulders.

"You're supposed to wait for me to say come in."

"And you're supposed to own a hotter swimsuit but here we are. Where did you get that unfortunate one-piece anyway, your grandmother?"

"I swam in high school. It's the only one I have."

"Your high school hated you."

I gave him the finger.

"Maybe just . . ." He reached over and began arranging my hair. "There. Now, no one will look at your suit."

I batted him away. "Thanks. I was really worried."

"You're welcome," he said, completely ignoring my sarcasm. "Ready?"

"Let's get this over with."

I led the way out, and we headed down the hall that would take us to the stairwell.

"You're a bucket of sunshine tonight," Milo said as we walked. "Did something happen?"

"Just the usual. No energy. No magic to help me ace this stuff. And no time to do anything about either one."

And still no idea who'd sent my mysterious letter.

"Sounds like what you need is to unwind." He pushed open the stairwell door, ushering me through. "Allow me."

I smirked. "Such a gentleman."

"Make sure to tell Cliff that, won't you?" He winked, and we climbed the stairs to the upper landing.

As we got close, I heard hushed voices.

At the top, Cliff and a half dozen other recruits stood huddled near a door with a keypad.

"Gem, glad you made it." Cliff glanced at Milo, who nudged me.

"This is Milo," I said.

"Hi." Milo shook Cliff's hand, lingering a little too long.

I rolled my eyes.

"Nice to meet you," Cliff said. "This is Leedle."

"Gem!" She high fived me.

"You two already know each other?" Cliff asked.

"We have Weapons Training together," I explained.

"Cool. This is Violet, Nate, Morgan, and Dutch."

"Hey," they all said.

I recognized Dutch from PT, but the others were unfamiliar.

"Nice to meet you," I said, offering a small wave.

Milo offered a charming smile, and then Cliff motioned for everyone to gather around the door.

"All right, let's go soak these sore muscles."

He input a series of numbers and the keypad beeped. He pulled the door open, and the others cheered.

"Ssh," Cliff said, and we all filed outside behind him.

The night air was crisp; chilled but not cold. I was glad for my one-piece.

"Perfect hot tub weather," Milo said, inhaling appreciatively.

I followed the others past an outdoor shower area and over to the far side of the roof where the hot tub was set up. From here, I could see the running track where I spent most mornings now. Just looking at the damned thing made my muscles hurt all over again.

"Water's perfect," Cliff said, easing in.

"This feels heavenly," Violet said. Her black hair was streaked with purple highlights that matched the shimmering highlights in her wings.

The others didn't waste time stripping down and stepping in, spreading out along the bench seating.

"You coming in?" Cliff asked me.

I peeled off my shirt and leggings and stepped into the heated water. My relief was instant.

I groaned as I slid lower. "Demon balls, that feels good."

Leedle snorted. "Preach."

"These workouts are hell," Cliff agreed.

"I'll take a workout over Rigo the Ego any day," Milo said.

Leedle snorted. "That is the perfect nickname for him."

"Well, perv would have been better, but it doesn't rhyme as well," Nate said.

Everyone agreed.

"Try pissing off Gorser the Enforcer," Cliff said with a grimace.

"Nicknames are contagious in this place," Milo said.

"Gorser. He's the Protocol and Procedures guy, right?" I asked.

Cliff nodded. "I have him for morning PT as well, and that guy loves burpees and suicides in a way that is not healthy."

Morgan and Nate muttered an agreement.

"Who do you have for PT?" Nate asked.

"Landis," I said, and Cliff groaned.

"She's so much easier."

"If someone could tell my thigh muscles that, I'd appreciate it," I said.

Milo smirked.

"Or Cliff could just massage those thighs instead."

I shot Milo a look. "I just thought of another nickname. Milo the Murdered."

His smirk vanished.

Leedle laughed, and Nate splashed her.

After that, the conversation veered off toward parties

and pizza and all the things we were missing by being locked away in here.

I gave Milo the hour I'd promised and then eased out of the tub. Grabbing my shirt, I used it as a towel before pulling it back on.

"Leaving so soon?"

I looked up at Cliff, who'd leaned over and propped his arm on the edge of the tub. It wasn't lost on me that somewhere during the past hour, Milo had slid in next to Dutch and Cliff had inched closer to me. In fact, his thigh brushing mine a moment ago had been the tipping point. The guy was nice enough but getting booted for fraternization wasn't on my list of things to do this week. Tony, Fiona, and others might have been able to get away with breaking that rule, but I knew better than to think I wasn't being scrutinized in a way the others weren't.

"I have a lot of reading to do," I said.

"Maybe I can help," Cliff said. "Split the work. You read half, I read half?"

Behind Cliff, I could see Milo giving me "the look," which was a universal nonverbal cue to "get laid, sista," but I ignored him.

"Maybe next time," I told him.

He flashed me a smile. "I look forward to it."

That's what I was afraid of.

"Hey, you want a chaperone to walk you back?" Milo asked as I pulled my joggers on over my wet suit.

"No, stay," I told him. "I'll see you tomorrow."

"Sweet dreams," he called as I slipped away.

The stairwell was dark, lit only by red exit signs on every floor. A flashlight, even the one on my cell, would have been nice. Or fae sight. But I had neither. Using the handle for reference, I went slowly until I reached the access door that led back to my dorm room.

The handle didn't budge.

I cursed silently as I realized they must have locked the doors for security purposes. Which meant Cliff was the only one with the damned code, and I was not going back up there to ask him for it. Not that I'd get back onto that roof anyway since it was locked now too.

Doubling back to the floor above, I tried the door there. Also locked.

Shit.

Descending again, I passed my floor and went all the way to the ground level. The instructor wing.

Of course that door opened right up.

I eased my head into the hall and looked right then left.

The sconces mounted to the walls cast the space into a yellowish haze. Nothing moved, and I slipped into the hall, carefully pulling the door shut behind me.

The soft click echoed in the silence. On its heels, I heard another noise. Small and far off, but definitely there.

My pulse sped.

Eyes scanning for movement, I hurried on.

If there was someone else moving around on this floor, all I had to do was get to the elevators. Being discovered there was an easy explanation compared to being caught wandering the staff quarters.

But three turns later, I knew I was lost.

The maze of halls was worse than my floor. At least there, signs pointed the way out. Down here, I was walking in circles for all I knew.

Behind me, something shuffled, and I turned, only to find the hall empty.

Doubling my pace, I made a left and then a right, hoping I'd changed it up from before.

This time, I heard distinct footsteps.

Again, I turned to look and found no one there.

"Oomph." I face-planted then quickly backed away when I realized I'd smacked into, not a wall, but a body.

I choked, swallowing my scream, and found myself eye level with a pair of the biggest nipples I'd ever seen.

"You not be here."

The voice was more of a throaty grunt than anything.

I looked up into the face of the same creature I'd seen the day I arrived. The ogre, though I still couldn't believe I was seeing one in real life.

"You're extinct," I blurted.

Cold fear washed over me as I realized I'd just run into the one creature I probably couldn't fool with reason. And I'd just insulted him.

The ogre's bushy eyebrows crinkled in confusion. "What . . . eshtinct?"

Relief. A second chance.

"Uh. It means . . . handsome."

His lips pulled back to reveal two rows of squared teeth, yellowed around the edges. I shrank back, wondering what it would feel like to get eaten by a creature whose teeth were as big as my fist.

"Ollie handsome." It took me a few seconds longer to realize he was smiling.

"Yeah." I forced a laugh. "Ollie handsome."

He grinned wider until I caught a glimpse into his cavernous mouth. My laughter abruptly died off.

His smile faded. The confusion returned.

"You teach to kill demon?"

"Uh, no, I'm a student here." Shit. This was the part where I needed to get creative with my story.

His friendly expression vanished. "You no be down here."

His voice boomed, and I couldn't believe no one came out into the hall to see what the noise was about.

"I know. I got lost." I forced my knees not to buckle as I imagined him picking me up and tossing me around like a doll in his too-big hands.

"You new."

It wasn't a question, but I nodded. "My name's Gem Hawkins."

Maybe if I told him my name he wouldn't eat me. Maybe ogres had a thing about eating food with names.

"Hawkins." His eyes lit up. "Vic Hawkins good friend."

"Vic was my dad. You knew him?"

"Vic Hawkins good friend," he repeated. "Vic bring me jerky."

I laughed. "You like jerky?"

"Ollie love goat jerky."

I tried not to wince. Dad had been a foodie beyond any human comprehension. As a supe, he prided himself on having tried all sorts of delicacies the humans deemed uncivilized.

"Goat jerky. Got it. Hey, maybe I can bring you some when I make detective."

Ollie shook his head. "No see me. Starla tell me always hide."

"The agency doesn't want anyone to know about you."

"Starla says Ollie special."

I smiled. "You are special, Ollie. I'm really glad I met you."

"Glad I met you, Gem Hawkins." He lifted his enormous hand, and I had to jump to reach for a high five.

I narrowly avoided face-planting into his hairy nipple when I landed. This whole magic-stripping thing was seriously dangerous.

"Well, I'm headed up to bed now," I said, and he nodded, pointing at the hall on my left.

"Elevator."

"Thanks," I told him and waved as I started off.

"Sleep tight." Ollie's voice echoed behind me, friendly but still. Coming from an ogre, it was also the most ominous thing I'd heard in a long time.

NINE

My legs burned, and my muscles screamed for relief. I grit my teeth, pushing with everything I had until the magic finally burst from my tired hands. Across the training arena, the demon howled as the ball of fire engulfed its slimy body. A moment later, the howling ceased and the demon melted into a pile of bright green goo.

From somewhere in the shadows of the balcony viewing area, a slow clap sounded.

I rolled my eyes.

I knew exactly who that clap belonged to. And the sarcasm behind it.

"Nice job, Hawkins." Rigo stepped forward and looked down at me, a nasty gleam in his eye. "Only took you twice as long as the others."

Irritation boiled up and over.

"Faith took almost twenty minutes and nearly burned

the place down," I called back. "I saw her limping to the nurse on her way out."

Faith. The brunette who'd lectured us during first-day orientation. She'd been just as annoying and brownnosing as I'd predicted. It didn't help that she was good—and I was constantly her runner-up.

Rodrigo's smile turned sour.

"My point is that you're improving, and that's in no small part thanks to my feedback. Without me, you'd have flunked out weeks ago."

This guy.

I bit back my retort and reminded myself I was almost there.

Four more weeks.

I only had four more weeks in this place. Then I was free.

"Fine. Any more feedback for me?" I asked, acid-sweetness dripping from my words.

Rodrigo responded by swinging his body over the railing and dropping to the training room floor. He strode over to me, arms swinging with whatever swagger he was attempting to exude.

I made sure to keep my face carefully blank.

He wanted a response. Any response. I'd learned that on day one. The same day Fiona had learned Rodrigo thought training us included touching us in places we hadn't asked to be touched.

Tony had threatened to kick his ass, but Fiona had insisted she could handle it.

She'd flunked out three and a half weeks ago.

Rigo claimed she'd failed an exam on evidence protocol. But I had a feeling she'd finally made it clear she wasn't interested in being teacher's pet. Since then, Rigo the Ego had made it a point to single me out. His behavior alternated between sleazy flirting and spiteful bullying. Sometimes both at once. It would have been impressive that he could pull off both at once—if it hadn't been so infuriating.

Now, his eyes flitted over my frame in a way that made my skin crawl. For weeks, I'd been reigning it in just enough to keep from earning his wrath. I was walking a fine line between outright refusal of his advances and landing a punch in his throat. But as graduation neared, he only got worse and maintaining my control only got harder.

Now, I fisted my hands, clenching my magic tight. Exhaustion or not, I would never *not* want to kick this guy's ass.

"You've gained weight," he said without a shred of propriety.

"I've gained muscle." I flashed him a feral smile.

He grunted then went back to perusing me like I was merchandise rather than an agent-in-training.

Where had they found this guy?

"You look tense. Here, let me."

His hands landed on my shoulders and began massaging. I jerked free the moment his hands began to move across my back and spun to face him.

"Don't touch me," I hissed, rage sending sparks of magic from my fingers.

His eyes widened.

"Whoa, cadet. Cool it," he ordered, his expression flashing with temper.

"Touch me again and I'll—"

"You'll what?" he demanded.

His eyes narrowed, and his smile curled confidently. Fur sprouted along his arms and face. His nose elongated into a snout and claws sprouted at the ends of his nails.

My nostrils flared with the scent of coyote in the air.

"Your words sound threatening, Hawkins. And you know how I feel about threats."

He drew a single claw along the underside of my chin. I grit my teeth to keep from outwardly wincing at the sting, refusing to budge. The feel of something wet trickled down my neck and underneath my shirt.

It took every ounce of self-control I had not to shift into something capable of ending him right where he stood.

But I could see the challenge in his eyes, the dare.

He wanted me to react so he could finally kick me out.

When I refused to take the bait, he dropped his hand and let his beast fade. Human once again, he smacked his tongue against his teeth and eyed me with a disgusting amount of confidence.

"That's all for today," he said finally. "Hit the showers. And let me know if you need any help."

His parting wink made me want to start over in my training simulation. With Rigo as the demon being incinerated.

Prick.

Magic roiling inside me, I marched off.

The moment I stalked out of the training room, my magic vanished. I blinked through the shock of it and waited for my body to adjust as I headed for my room. I pressed a hand to the scratch Rodrigo had left behind. He wanted me to go running to the clinic and rat him out, but I wasn't interested in petty revenge.

Instead, I wiped away the blood and headed for the showers.

Rage pumped through me, chasing the adrenaline left behind by my need to defend myself. I had to cool it, to keep from doing something stupid. I had to calm my emotions enough to keep from tracking down Rigo and feeding his testicles to him through a straw.

I needed a reminder about why I was really here.

Alone in my room, I pulled out the cell phone that would get me booted if anyone ever found it. When I was sure I was in the clear, I powered it on and hit play on the message.

"Hey, Gem. It's Dad. Listen, I don't think I'll make it to dinner after all. I have a meeting that's run late, and I can't leave with this last thing still on my plate. I'll make it up to you tomorrow. Maybe we can do the beignet binge challenge. I know your mother hates that." Laughter. "Okay, I gotta run, but I'll call you in the morning, and we'll make a plan. Love you, beastie."

The call ended.

I hit the button to replay it again.

And again.

And again.

A few minutes later, I shut the phone off again and stowed the phone back in its hiding spot. I had no doubt there was some kind of spellwork in place to detect calls, incoming or outgoing. But nothing stood in the way of listening to old voice mails. Or at least, no one had come barging in to bust me for it yet, so I assumed.

Someone knocked, startling me. I swiped quickly at my wet cheeks and wondered if maybe I'd been wrong about the spell detecting my phone.

"Come in."

The door opened, and Milo walked in.

I blew out a breath.

"How'd it go?" he asked.

"The first thing I'm doing when I graduate is having a voodoo doll made of Rigo's dick," I announced.

"And the second thing?"

"I'm going to feed the voodoo doll to a meat grinder."

He winced. "That bad, huh?"

I sighed. "It was fine. I aced it. I mean, Rigo the Ego still found a way to be a sleaze, but I passed."

He lowered himself onto the desk chair—the only other space to sit in the small room. "We expect nothing less from that guy. As far as the test, that's good news. What's wrong?"

"Nothing. I just . . ."

Milo was the closest thing to a friend I'd made in here. But even he didn't know everything. It wasn't personal. Over the last couple of months, he'd more than proven he could keep a secret.

It was more about me not wanting to say the words aloud. Words like: *my dad's dead, and I think the SSF knows who killed him but is covering it up.* And *someone— possibly an agent—is trying to scare me into silence.*

Those were words better left unsaid—at least while we were still inside the walls of the Tiff.

"My ex came looking for me, and Starla pulled me aside for questioning."

Milo's eyes went wider than I'd ever seen. "Are you kidding me?"

I shook my head.

"When?"

"A couple of weeks ago," I admitted.

"And you're just now telling me?"

"For your own protection," I said.

"I can handle a secret, Gem Hawkins." He arched a brow. "I think I've proven that already."

"You have. Sorry. I'm just not used to having someone to tell."

He studied me. "You strike me as the type to not let people in so easily."

I shrugged. "I've got a lot to lose."

"Maybe. But there's a flip side."

"What's that?"

"You also have a lot to gain. If you choose wisely."

I smirked. "Let me guess. You're the wise choice."

"You could do a lot worse."

"I have," I admitted, and he leaned in, eyes wide.

"Do tell."

"Z, the guy who came looking for me, was nothing but trouble." I blew out a breath. "You would have loved him."

"Nah." Milo shook his head. "If he hurt you, I'm not interested."

I was struck by his words. When was the last time I'd had a friend like Milo? Lila, maybe, but she was human. There was only so much I shared with her. Only so far I let her in.

Dad.

He'd been my last true confidant. The last creature in the world to truly understand me.

"Thanks, Milo," I said quietly.

Moisture stung my eyes.

Milo squeezed my shoulders.

"Don't mention it. This place is a hellhole of stress." Milo stood and rubbed his hands together, breaking up the emotional moment. It was more proof he was a great friend because the last thing I intended to do was let this mushiness drag on. "Did you eat dinner at least?"

"First dinner, yes."

He grinned.

"Perfect. Tony just asked my advice about how to win over Fiona when he gets home, and I need to eat my feelings."

"Milo." Sympathy softened me.

"Second dinner's on me. Come on." He tapped my foot as he rose and led the way out.

"Dinner's free here, you tool."

"Well then, I'll carry your tray."

"My hero." I snorted and pulled my door shut behind me as we headed for the dining hall.

TEN

"Detectives make decent money," Tony said as I sat down with my burger and fries after a long day of training.

"Paying us well is the least they can do considering all the shit we'll take from the rest of our kind," Milo pointed out.

Tony didn't argue.

We all knew what it would be like for us out there once we graduated. Half the supe population was like Faith: loyal and supportive of the agency who worked to keep the planet safe from monsters. The other half still harbored resentment for an organization that had a history of marginalizing the misunderstood and persecuting anything perceived as a threat. They'd done more than their share to pit supes against one another over the years.

"Whatever," Tony said, waving off Milo's negativity. "My point is this job will give me the means to get up and out. That's what matters. When I'm out of here, I'm renting an apartment. Something with my name on the lease. Something no one can take from me."

"That's a good plan," I said.

"What about you?" he asked.

"Nissan GT-R. Nismo. Royal blue." I almost drooled thinking about it.

Tony grinned. "Does the club know you plan to ditch their Acura line?"

"The club probably thinks I deserted," I said with a shrug.

"You didn't tell them you were recruited?" he asked.

"My mechanic knows, but he's sworn to secrecy. The supes around that scene aren't exactly the kind who would support this career choice," I said. "Not to mention, my badge will mean I can bust them for illegal racing when I get out of here."

"Good point," he agreed.

"Next you'll tell me you joined up just to get out of all the speeding tickets," Milo said.

"It doesn't hurt," I admitted.

Tony grinned. "The perks of law enforcement, eh?"

I grinned back. "Damn right."

Milo rolled his eyes. "You guys are ridiculous."

"Don't give me those judgy eyes," I said. "You're the one who told me you're going to use your badge to cancel your parking ticket debt."

"That meter maid has it out for me."

Tony and I shared a look.

"Fine," Milo said. "If you must know, I also plan to use my badge to intimidate all the little shits who think they run my neighborhood."

"Your badge doesn't get you off the hook for beating up little kids," I warned.

"No, but it lets me confiscate their booze and e-cigs, and that's basically the same thing."

"Hey, Hawkins."

I looked up at the sound of my name. "Yeah?"

Desmond, a broad-shouldered werewolf, nodded at me, a tray balanced in one hand as he passed our table. I recognized him from my demon-hunting class. We hadn't talked much, but then I wasn't much for talking when I could be working toward proving myself.

"Nice job in the arena today. That Brax demon was no joke, but you handled yourself."

"Thanks."

The guy lingered like he wanted to say more then finally sauntered off.

Milo rolled his eyes at me.

"What?" I demanded.

"He likes you," Milo said.

"Desmond?" I frowned. "He was just congratulating me on not getting impaled by a razor claw. I hardly think that means he's smitten."

KISS OF DEATH   125

"First of all, no one says smitten anymore."

I scoffed, but Milo looked to Tony for confirmation.

"He's right," Tony said around a mouthful of steak.

"Whatever. Desmond's just a friend," I said.

"But he could be more," Milo said.

"Could be but won't," I said.

"Have you taken a vow of celibacy I don't know about?" Milo demanded.

"No. I just have other priorities right now."

"Like finding out who killed your dad?" Tony asked.

I frowned. "How do you know about that?"

Tony hesitated.

"Sweetie, everyone knows about that," Milo said gently.

I sighed. He was right. I was the one pretending here. Gossip was bound to have circulated by now. I saw it in the way the other instructors treated me. Some had singled me out, calling on me for answers more than the others. Most had overcompensated by ignoring me. A couple of them, like Kinrade, had made it clear they didn't plan to let me through on my father's reputation alone and had given me extra homework almost every day now.

Fine by me. I was nearly top of my class with or without my dad's legacy. And I didn't care how the other students saw me, but it wasn't fair to keep lying to my friends.

"The truth is my dad was murdered, and the report

they gave was a joke. Every time I pushed for more, they fed me a line and then went back to ignoring the whole thing. So, I decided to get answers for myself."

"That's why you joined the agency," Milo said. "For its resources."

"And to get access to the people who knew him," I admitted, thinking of Raphziel. Not that *he'd* ever give me the answers I wanted.

"Damn, it's a long game you're playing." Tony said the words like they were a warning.

"I've got time. My dad didn't though, and I think there's someone out there who knows what really happened."

"I'm sorry about your dad, Gem," Milo said. "It must have been really hard."

"My mom took it pretty rough," I said. "Losing her mate has really been hard on her. Knowing what happened will help ease some of it. For both of us."

"I get it," Milo said. "My mom had it rough when my old man left, and he was just a human with a commitment problem. Fae mating bonds are intense."

"Family's important," Tony agreed. "My sister's all I've got, but I'd do anything for her. Including slaying some demons."

"Thanks for understanding," I told them.

"But listen," Milo continued, "You can't just give up

living your life. I didn't know your dad, but I doubt he would want that for you."

"I'm not giving up," I said.

"Bull shit. What about the driving?" Milo challenged.

"I can always go back to that."

"And all your friends? Aren't there people you left behind?"

"I have Lila, my boss at the Sandwich Shop," I admitted. "But it's not like I'll never see her again. In fact, it's safer this way. If I never eat another sandwich, I'll die happy."

"What do you have against sandwiches?" Milo asked.

"Have you ever tried a molasses turkey melt on waffle bread?"

Milo made a face. "I think I'll pass."

Tony rubbed his chin. "I wouldn't mind it."

"Even better," I said. "I volunteer you to be her guinea pig next time she asks."

"Cool." He nodded.

I laughed and went back to my veggie burger, glad we'd moved back toward a less serious topic.

When I looked up again, Milo was watching me with narrowed eyes.

"What?" I demanded.

"Two more males just walked by and checked you out like they were on a deserted island and you were a last meal."

"For the last time, I'm not interested. And stop looking at me like that," I said.

"I can't help it. I've never seen someone so averse to getting laid before."

Tony snorted.

I glared at them both. "I don't know, you two seem to be giving me a run for my money."

Milo scowled.

"We don't get outside privileges for another month," Tony pointed out.

I gestured to the crowded dining hall. "Plenty of choices right here."

Milo looked at Tony longingly.

Tony shook his head. "Not happening. Fraternizing among recruits will get you booted."

"Exactly," I pointed out. "Which is why Desmond is—"

"Green." Milo's expression froze as he stared out ahead.

"What?" I frowned. "No, he's off-limits—"

"No, he's literally *green*. What the hell?"

I followed his horrified gaze and saw Desmond standing two tables over. He clawed at his arms, which were currently lime green, his eyes wide in horror.

Another recruit stood and said something to him, but Desmond shook his head and backed away. A staff member approached but Desmond shouted at him then turned and ran from the dining hall.

The staff member hurried after him.

Everyone stared in silence at the door Desmond had exited.

Slowly, the quiet that had fallen over the room was replaced with a growing hum of voices.

I looked back at Milo and Tony, all three of us wearing matching faces of confusion.

"Does anyone know what the hell just happened?" Milo asked.

Tony and I both shook our heads.

"I can't say I've ever seen that before," I said.

But Tony's confusion shifted toward contemplation. His brow furrowed.

"What is it?" Milo prompted.

"Not sure. I saw something on Professor Wayne's desk the other day. Some internal memo regarding the city's demon activity."

"What does the city's demon activity have to do with Desmond turning green?"

"I don't know," Tony admitted. "Most of the report was redacted. But from what I could gather, there was some incident involving an undocumented demon. The agent who went up against it exhibited strange symptoms in the weeks following."

"What kind of symptoms?" I asked.

"Some behavioral stuff. Paranoia and mood swings. But the report also listed skin discolorations."

"What kind of demon was it?" I asked, intrigued.

"It didn't say. Or if it did, that part had been classified."

"You still have a copy of the article?" I asked.

"I can get it."

"Mind if I take a look?"

He shrugged. "Sure. But there isn't much else legible besides what I've just told you."

"Maybe there's a reference listed that'll tell us where we can find out more," I said.

Or maybe my fae magic could un-redact some of it— like I'd done with my father's investigation reports. I didn't want to get their hopes up though. Especially since even attempting that would mean doing it under the noses of our instructors—which was the only time they gave us our magic back long enough for me to try.

"I don't get it," Milo said. "The only demons we train with here are level three and below. In the last eighteen months, only a handful of fours and fives have been spotted anywhere in the country. And none of them have the power to turn a guy green." He turned to me. "You said you guys trained on a Brax demon today?"

"Yeah. But Desmond didn't have contact with it. Far as I could tell, he put the thing down with his magic from ten feet away."

"Guess it's a mystery." He shot me a look. "Unless you

decided to ask him directly." He smirked. "I bet he'd tell you."

"First, you assume I care enough to find out."

His eyes gleamed with smugness. "Of course you care. It's about demons. And agents. And possible conspiracies. This is right up your alley."

Dammit, he was right.

"Fine," I said. "I'll talk to Desmond."

Milo grinned. "I knew it."

"Ugh. You're such a pain in the ass when you're right."

AFTER DINNER, I asked around and found Desmond's room farther down my own hallway. I knocked but no one answered. Looking around to be sure the coast was clear, I turned the knob and poked my head inside. The bed sat unmade and clothes littered the floor. No sign of Desmond.

Returning to my room, I kept my door open and one eye on the recruits that passed through our hall, but Desmond never passed by. The more I thought about what had happened in the dining hall, the less it made sense. No one had ever reported skin changes caused by demon contact. Poison, yes. Slime, sure. Lizard-skin, no.

It didn't add up.

First thing the next morning, I made my way to the clinic and found Leslie at her desk.

"Hi, Gem. What can I do for you? Feeling all right?"

"Feeling great. I was wondering about another recruit who came in last night. Desmond Ayers."

She smiled blankly. "I'm not sure I know that name. Is he a new recruit?"

"Uh, not really. He's been here as long as I have. His skin turned green during dinner last night. I assumed he came to see you."

"Green? Well, that is memorable. But I'm afraid he didn't come through the clinic. I was here all night and only treated a mild headache for one of the female recruits."

I tried to think of where else Desmond would have gone in his state, but nothing came to mind.

"Right, I'm sure I'm just confused," I said, and Leslie smiled as I let myself out.

The rest of my day was packed with physical conditioning and weapons instruction. Desmond wasn't in the training arena that afternoon, and I finally got curious enough to track down Rodrigo to ask about him. I waited until after class, making sure to note what kind of demons everyone was paired with and what elimination methods they used to take them out.

None of the demons were known for causing skin problems.

When class ended, I hung back and waited until the others had mostly filed out before catching up with Rodrigo.

"Hey, I was wondering about Desmond Ayers," I said.

"What about him?" Rodrigo's eyes lingered on my fitted tank, and I bit back irritation.

"He turned green at dinner last night," I said pointedly.

Rodrigo's eyes snapped to mine. Carefully blank. "Right. He ate something that didn't sit well and got a little sick. He's fine now."

"He wasn't in class all day," I pointed out.

"A day in the clinic. Doctor's orders."

"Funny. I was there this morning and the place was empty. Leslie never saw him."

Rodrigo's eyes narrowed as he snapped, "The status of another recruit is none of your business, Hawkins. Eyes on your own paper, understand?"

"What kind of demon can turn a person green?" I pushed.

Rodrigo's face reddened, and I knew I'd gone too far.

"Maybe you're not hearing me, recruit." His mouth cinched into a hard line. "Tell you what, you can spend the next week working the kitchen line. Maybe that'll give you a better understanding of how much our food choices affect our bodies."

My shoulders slumped.

His gaze roamed my body in a way that made my skin crawl. "Of course your meals have already done your body good."

I rolled my eyes. "I'll report to the kitchen."

His mouth lifted in invitation. "You're welcome to work off your community service another way if you prefer."

I pinned him with a hard look and swallowed back all the vile words I didn't dare say for fear of getting booted. "I'd rather turn green."

ELEVEN

A week later, my kitchen penance was complete but Desmond still hadn't returned. Tony's redacted memo provided little else in the way of information; even my fae magic couldn't reveal what the agency gurus had apparently worked so hard to hide.

I focused on training, but every night before bed, I pulled out my contraband phone and listened to the last voice mail my father ever sent. I was still no closer to figuring out what really happened but listening to his voice reminded me why I'd come. And why I was putting up with all the bull shit that came with becoming an agent.

Halfway through the message, my door opened and Milo walked in.

I paused the audio and slid the phone quickly away. "This isn't what it looks like."

"That's funny. Because it looks like you smuggled in a

cell phone and use it to replay your dad's last voice mail before he died."

"Okay, fine." I blew out a breath. "It's exactly what it looks like. But I haven't made any calls out, I swear."

"Relax. I'm not going to tell anyone about your phone. It's not like I haven't known about it for weeks anyway."

My eyes widened. "You knew? How?"

"Gem, darling, you continue to underestimate me." He sat on my bed and tossed a file at me. "Here. I brought you a present."

"What's this?"

"Open it and find out."

I peeled open the file, and my eyes widened as I read the contents.

"This is the memo Tony gave me," I said, noting the familiar headline. Then my eyes caught on the rest of it. "It's unredacted."

"You're welcome," Milo said with a self-satisfied smirk.

I looked down at the report again, and sure as shit, the blackout had been removed to reveal the full report. "How did you do it?"

He shrugged. "I know people."

"Uh-huh." Clearly, considering fae magic hadn't been enough to lift the spell hiding the words.

I studied him closer.

"*Why* did you do it?"

"I don't like what happened to Desmond, but I don't

like what happened to your dad even more. You're sad, Gem. Grieving. And my heart hurts for you." He shrugged. "I wanted to help."

I bit my lip, touched by how much he'd noticed, especially when I'd done my best to hide it from them all.

"I'm sorry I haven't talked about it," I said quietly.

"You have nothing to apologize for. Anyway, since I can't help ease that pain, I wanted to help solve the mystery of what happened to Desmond. And look at the third paragraph down. I think what's in that report might shed some light on what we saw."

I scanned the write-up quickly, my shock growing with each new sentence.

When I was done, I looked up at Milo with wide eyes.

"This could change everything," I said.

He nodded, his usual cheerful expression full of warning.

"This proves there are uncatalogued demons," he said. "Creatures we've never seen before. And the agency knows about them."

"One of them got to Desmond," I said, noting the article's write-up about an unknown demon whose touch turned its victims green.

"It doesn't say whether the effects are reversible, but it does explain what we saw."

"Milo, this is . . . I don't know what to say."

"You don't need to say anything. I just wanted you to know you can trust me."

I blinked back a sheen of tears. "I do trust you. And I do want to say something. Actually, I want to tell you everything."

In a quiet voice, I told him what had happened to my father, including the agency's reaction to it all.

"They tried to tell you a level one had taken him out?" he said when I got to the part about the bogus reports they gave us.

"Not only was my dad way too good at his job to get taken out by a non-lethal demon, he didn't have a mark on him when they found his body."

"What do you mean? No bites?"

"No bites, no stab wounds, no broken skin. Nothing."

"That doesn't make sense. Every known demon uses violent force to kill."

"Exactly. Nothing about it adds up."

"And that's why you became an agent."

I nodded. "Someone in the agency knows the truth."

"You could have told me all this before, you know. I feel like an asshole for teasing you so much about getting laid when you were over here trying to solve a cover-up."

"I guess I just found it easier to keep it all inside. But I do trust you, and I really appreciate this."

"For you, lover, anytime." He winked, and I offered a wobbly smile.

"I mean it, Milo. I haven't had a friend I could share this stuff with. . .well, ever."

"That's because you hadn't met me yet."

"You're absolutely one of a kind," I said, and he grinned.

"Don't you forget it. Also, I'm still going to tease you about getting laid because life's simple joys are what make it worth living."

I groaned and looked at the report again, frowning as the truth of what the agency had hidden finally began to sink in.

"I can't believe there are undocumented demons in our city," I said.

"Oh, shit, I just remembered. Look," Milo said, flipping through and pulling out a photo of a dead agent. According to the report, the man had been found alone and without any outward sign of injury. No demon in sight.

"They're calling it a mentocule demon," Milo said. "What's that?"

"No idea." I scanned the page for a description, but there were no other details beyond the name of the demon.

"There's gotta be somewhere we can look for more info on these assholes."

My eyes widened. "Hang on, I have an idea."

I jumped up and grabbed the book Professor Kinrade had assigned me.

"What's this?"

"Kinrade insisted I read it for extra credit," I said, flipping through the glossary of creatures.

"I thought you were acing her class."

"I am."

"Then why do you need extra credit?"

"I don't." When he only looked more confused, I sighed. "I'm a legacy. For the teachers here, that means making my life harder than everyone else's. I've had extra homework in nearly every single unit we've covered."

"Are you saying the professors give you more work than everyone else?"

"That's exactly what I'm saying."

"That's unfair."

"Believe me, I agree. Write your congressman or something, because no one here gives a rat's ass about fair."

He snorted.

I found the page number for mentocule and flipped through until I found the correlating section.

"Look. It says mentocule demons can kill without touch using telepathic radio waves and—shit! They're a level seven?"

"What?" Milo grabbed the book and leaned in to read where I'd pointed. "Holy Hellfire. I didn't even know sevens existed."

"Neither did I."

We were both silent as we read the scant paragraph

about the mentocule demon. There wasn't much in the text, but what was there blew my mind.

Milo looked just as stunned.

"Gem, it says the mentocule can kill without piercing its victims skin. Just like—"

"My dad," I breathed.

"This is crazy. They're literally in here teaching us everything above a level three is extinct."

"Who else knows about this? Who wrote the article?"

Flipping through the papers, I noted the clearance level on the reports. They were designated "for Neph eyes only." No wonder no one here had been able to tell me what really happened to Desmond.

Where names would have been listed, there were only blank spaces. The heading underneath the blank space categorized the recipient as simply "Nephilim."

"Who else has seen this?" I asked.

"Unredacted? No one. I swiped it from Wayne before he even read it," Milo said.

"How did he get it?"

Milo shrugged. "No idea."

I shook my head. "They're hiding the truth from everyone," I realized. "Even their own agents."

"That's weird." Milo picked up one of the reports and studied it closer, frowning.

"What?"

"None of the reports list a Neph superior."

"Why is that weird?"

"We talked about it during our protocol lecture last week. If it's classified to the highest level, one of the council members has to be listed. Look, this is where it would usually give a name."

He pointed to a space on the report that was still redacted.

"How did this redaction remain intact when you cleared the rest of it?"

"Hmm." Milo's brows wrinkled in confusion. "The spell should have removed all the magic," he said almost to himself.

"How did you remove the redaction, anyway?" I asked. "I tried everything and couldn't crack it."

Milo shot me a crooked smile. "I might have traded favors with Professor Wayne."

My jaw dropped. "You slept with Professor Wayne?"

"What? Underneath that Hawaiian shirt, he's a DILF."

"What's a DILF?"

"Dad I'd like to fu—"

"Got it. Ugh." I squeezed my eyes shut. "That is an image I did not need."

"You asked," he said, snickering.

He was enjoying this way too much.

"Okay, seriously, we really need to have a conversation about your lack of boundaries."

"I have boundaries," he said. "They're just a lot more flexible than yours. With doors and gates. That are unlocked. And open windows. With signs that say 'Come inside.'"

"No more sleeping with teachers," I said.

"How about no more sleeping with teachers at the Tiff? There's a librarian at my little cousin's school who is just delicious—"

"Aghh. How about no more sex talk for tonight instead?"

He grinned. "Deal."

TWELVE

"Holy shit, why is it so crowded in here?" Milo complained as he wedged himself and his dinner tray into his usual spot.

"New group of trainees came in," Tony said.

"There's, like, a million supes in here." Milo elbowed the guy on his left, ignoring the scowl he earned.

"I heard the new crowd has to double bunk," Tony said. "All the dorms are full. And the showers? Forget it."

"Why are they bringing in so many?" I asked.

"Demons are on the rise." I looked over at the girl who'd spoken up. She sat next to Tony and had broken off her conversation with her friends to answer. A pair of stubby horns protruded from the front of her head.

"What do you mean?" I asked. "The numbers have been holding steady for years now."

Her brows crinkled in confusion. "Yeah, of course. I mean, until the past couple of months."

None of us answered.

Milo and I exchanged a look.

"Don't you guys watch the news?" the girl asked.

"Not in here," Tony said.

"Not allowed," Milo put in.

"Right. Well, there's an increase in demon activity in the city," she explained. "The SSF is recruiting the largest wave of new agents in a hundred years or something crazy. Signing bonuses too."

"What?" Milo demanded. He looked at Tony and me. "We didn't get shit."

She shrugged. "It was either that or a supernatural draft."

"What kind of demons are being reported?" I asked her.

"Mostly level threes. But I heard my dad talking a few weeks back to the wolf shifter rep for our borough, and there's some chatter about a four out near the river. Probably gossip but still. Job security, right?"

"Right," I muttered, thinking of that report. And of Desmond.

"Welcome to the ranks," Tony said to her.

"Thanks." She grinned. "I've always wanted to be an agent, but with the demons under control, it was so hard to get accepted. This was my third application. It's so exciting."

"So exciting," Milo repeated.

I could hear the sarcasm dripping, but the girl either didn't notice or didn't care. She flashed another smile and then turned back to her friends, tuning us out once again.

"This is bull shit," Milo hissed. "These newbies all get signing bonuses? What about us? We were here before it was cool again."

"We're almost out of here, and that's bonus enough for me," I said.

"Can't argue there," Tony agreed. "First thing I'm doing after graduation is taking Fiona out on a proper date."

"First thing I'm doing is the hottest guy at Govenchy's Club," Milo said dreamily.

I shook my head.

"What about you, Gem?" Tony asked. "What's the first thing you'll do with freedom?"

I hesitated, actually thinking about my answer. "If you'd asked me that three months ago, I probably would have said buy a new car or a nicer apartment, but I don't think those are me anymore."

"What's your answer now?" Milo asked.

"I don't know. Nothing about my old life waits for me out there."

They fell silent, their expressions matching shades of concern.

"That's a little bleak," Tony said finally.

I shrugged. "When we graduate, we become agents—which means we officially belong to the SSF. What's free about that?"

"We work for them, sure, but we're still our own people," Tony said.

"Are we?"

I shook my head, pushing my food around on my plate. Somewhere along the way, my grief and anger had given way to something bigger. I thought about the report Milo had revealed. Undocumented demons. Dead agents. And lies to cover it up. Whatever was going on wasn't happening *to* the SSF. It was happening because of them.

Had Dad known that when he died?

Was that what his "big find" had been?

The more I thought about it, the more convinced I became that it was all connected. Dad's death. The increased number of demons. The recruits they'd hired to fight them.

Milo and Tony and the others might look at graduation as the end goal, but I knew better. The day we left these walls for the outside world was the day the real fight would begin.

MY ARMS ACHED thanks to the weight of the rebar I'd been swinging for the past hour. Sweat had plastered my shirt to my skin, and I'd already found a second wind. Then a third. I was working my way through wind number four when the buzzer finally sounded, signaling the end of the training simulation.

There was a collective groan that echoed off the high walls as the other recruits dropped their weapons and shuffled back toward the center of the arena.

I caught sight of Faith approaching from the far end. Her clothes were smooth, her perfect hair un-mussed. But she looked way too confident to have been anything but successful. Sure enough, one of the instructors patted her on the back as she passed. She smiled graciously and then waited until his back was turned to flip me off.

Bitch.

Tony and Milo were already there when I reached the group. Tony had a shallow cut on his cheek, and Milo looked like he'd been through some kind of dust storm.

"You look like shit," Milo said to me.

"You say the sweetest things." I batted my lashes at him, and Tony snorted.

"What happened to your knuckles? Did you punch a wall?" he demanded.

"A fennec demon, actually."

"Those are demon guts on your hand?" he screeched loudly enough that others turned.

Professor Thorne strode up. For the last few weeks, my class had combined with another and the professors were doubling up to accommodate the new wave of students. I wasn't complaining. Professor Thorne was tough, but with her around, Rigo had been slightly less sleazy.

She grabbed my hand and frowned as she inspected it. "You'll live," she announced flatly and then marched away to address the class.

"Today was a great test of street skill," Professor Thorne informed the group. "From our observation decks, we were able to see the improvisation you all displayed. Weapons were forged in the moment, and you all used everything from repurposed metal to a hanging plant to disable the enemy. Overall, very impressive."

"A hanging plant?" I whispered.

"Guilty," Tony muttered.

I muffled a laugh.

"Improvising with weaponry and strategy is your best chance at survival," Professor Thorne went on. "Now, the following students are dismissed and will report back tomorrow for a secondary test. If you pass that, you go on to your final exam. If not, you will get one more shot at this.

Those who fail to complete their last mission will be eliminated or assigned to a support position with the agency."

I tensed.

Milo and Tony stilled, and the rest of the students fell silent as we all waited for the names to be called.

"Faith Greene, Brent Trettel, Milo Mercer, and Gemini Hawkins. Please report back tomorrow for the partnered portion of your exam."

My relief was short-lived as Professor Thorne ended the session and Tony's face fell. The other students broke apart and headed for the showers. I hung back with Milo and Tony.

"Fucking hanging basket," Tony muttered. "I should have gone for the broken bottle."

"It's not a big deal," Milo said, clapping him on the back. "You'll get it next time."

"If there *is* a next time," Tony said.

THIRTEEN

Darkness hung over the entire alley like a curtain. I knew because I'd put it there. My magic hummed like a song being quietly played in the background. Like the sound-track to my new life, I realized. If it were a radio station, it would be goth punk grunge. Angry. Loud. Without any discernible words.

"What about Phillip?" Milo asked.

The question distracted me from my music-as-life's-soundtrack imaginings. I cut Milo a look.

"No."

"Why not? He's polite and very athletic and really freaking hot."

"Because I'm not dating, that's why."

He huffed.

I ignored it.

"Okay, how about Faith instead?" I swung a look at

Milo, who shrugged. "Look, all I'm saying is if you're batting for the other team, you can tell me."

"I'm not batting for any team. Ugh. Can we just kill this demon and get back to campus? I'm starving."

"Fine. But let it go on the record that you're not very fun in the field, Gem Hawkins."

I didn't argue.

I wasn't trying to be fun. I was trying to be good at this. At least I hadn't gotten paired with Faith.

And I was currently outside the walls of the Tiff. That was something I could appreciate—even if we were stuck out near the docks far away from so much as a scent of the city.

Professor Thorne and Rigo had given us GPS coordinates and instructions to hunt down and destroy whatever demons were camped out down here. If we succeeded, we passed this test. This late in the training process, failure meant being sent home.

That wasn't an option.

With renewed focus, I motioned for Milo to follow me. The river was just ahead, and while our current location was several miles outside of the city, I knew this area well. Dad and I had come out here often in recent years, spending afternoons navigating from the rooftops above or shifting into griffins and taking to the skies. He'd always point out demon evidence, showing me how to track them properly. As I'd gotten older, he'd even shown me how to kill them. But only as my beast.

Being here now brought back so many memories, and I shoved them away, determined to focus on the assignment instead.

Milo and I walked in silence for several minutes, both of us using our supe senses to detect the location of our prey.

A buzzing sound interrupted the stillness and we both jerked our heads toward the noise.

Milo leaned in to swat at the bug headed straight for my face.

"Back off, fuckshuttle!"

A beetle slammed into my cheek.

I jerked aside, rubbing my stinging skin.

"Gran?"

"Well, it ain't the Pope."

The June bug dropped into my open palm, and Milo's jaw fell open.

"That bug just talked."

"I'm not a bug, you lintlicker," Gran retorted.

Milo's eyes widened. "I stand corrected. That bug just talked *shit*."

"Gran, what are you doing here?" I glanced around for some sign that Rigo or Professor Thorne had decided to track our progress. So far, we were alone, but who knew how long that would last.

"I was cruising around at the docks for fresh shipments of mustard greens," Gran said. She looked at Milo. "They're my favorite, you know."

"Uh, of course." Milo blinked.

"Anywho, I heard you two chatting, and I said to myself, 'I'd know that voice anywhere.' So I hightailed it over, and sure as shitnuggets, it's my beautiful granddaughter and her devilishly handsome new beau."

"Milo is not my beau, Gran."

"But he is devilishly handsome," Milo put in.

"Gran, you can't be here," I said. "We're in the middle of a test right now."

"Oh, are you slaying a demon down here?" Her wings buzzed as she lifted high enough to fly in a circle so she could scan the area.

"Yes, and we have to do it alone. If our professors find out you were here, they might fail us," I told her.

"Not to mention, they'd have questions." Milo arched a brow. "I mean, *I* have questions."

"Don't we all, son." Gran turned back to me. "How's the school thing going? You whooping ass?"

"I'm getting close to graduation," I said.

"And she's whooping ass," Milo put in.

"Hot dog, that's what I like to hear." Gran flitted closer to Milo. "You are a bite of deliciousness. Whew, if I had a working vagina—"

"Gran!"

Milo's cheeks puffed out as he attempted to hold back his laughter.

"I need to focus," I told her. "How's Mom?"

"Your momma's just fine. Been eating good what with the casseroles from the neighbors. Oh, and that mechanic stopped by."

"Juice? That's good."

"Oh and that Neph mouthbreather is really trying my patience."

"Wait. Neph?" I stilled. "You've seen Nephilim? At the house?"

"Yeah, that feisty bugger from your dad's funeral."

"There was a Nephilim at your dad's funeral?" Milo asked, looking impressed.

"Raph?" I asked, ignoring Milo.

"That's the one. He brought her flowers." Gran made a gagging sound.

"Is she vomiting?" Milo asked.

"That little homewrecker makes me sick," she spat.

"Gran, I need you to try and figure out what Raph wants with Mom, okay?"

Gran huffed. "I think you and I both know what he—"

"Besides that," I said, pinching the bridge of my nose. This day had taken a turn, and I really needed to right this train before it derailed completely. "Neph don't fraternize with supes. You know that. He has to want something else from her. I need you to find out what, okay?"

"You want me to do some agency shenanigans? Some recon?"

"Yes, can you do that?"

"You bet your sweet cheeks I can."

Her wings fluttered, and she lifted into the air. Then she almost tumbled before righting herself again.

"Tried saluting. Keep forgetting I don't have hands. Anywho, I'm going to sign off. Over and out. Roger, Roger."

I shook my head. "Bye Gran. I love you. Be careful."

"Tootaloo."

When she was gone, I looked at Milo.

His expression was frozen in amused confusion.

"Care to explain that?"

"My Gran is a shapeshifter, like me," I said. "When my grandpa Cal died last year, she took it hard, and her grief affected her magic. She shifted into a June bug and hasn't been able to change since."

"You're saying she's stuck like that?"

"So far."

He blinked at me. "And I thought my family was crazy."

I rolled my eyes. "Come on. Let's just get this done already."

Turning back in the direction of our coordinates, I concentrated, magic at the ready. We didn't have much farther to go.

From somewhere among the stacked shipping containers, I caught the sensation of a presence that went far beyond human or even supe.

I stilled.

"Do you smell it?" I whispered.

"Smells like ass-sweat and tomatoes," Milo said.

I decided not to ask about the tomatoes part.

Together, we started forward, creeping between containers until the path narrowed.

From the depths of the alley came a shuffle.

Milo and I shared another look. Considering the glamour spell I'd woven to keep anything human out, there was only one thing that could possibly be making a noise like that.

It was go time.

With a subtle head nod and a quick hand gesture, I sent Milo around to guard my flank and started forward again.

Milo sank into the shadows until he was longer visible. Even to my fae eyes, he was just gone.

Moving silently, I crept to the back of the alley and rounded the corner. A trail of goo greeted me. By the angel, tracking these things was so easy, it was stupid.

The slimy ribbon led to a door hanging open on the back end of the building. I kept my movements measured and silent as I sucked my body in tight and slid in through the opening.

Another noise. A scuffling and then a high-pitched squeak.

Rata demons were gross and possibly the most annoying of the monsters that roamed this planet. But they weren't gooey as far as I knew. So where the hell was the slime coming from?

I crept warily through the space, eyes sharp for some sign of my quarry.

The building had once been a print mill but now sat rotting and infested with the kind of rodent demons that thrived in damp, dark places humans had forgotten.

The smell hit me first, and I tensed, ready to blast the first scuttling thing I saw.

In the corner, something moved.

A squeak sounded.

Milo burst through the door behind me, unleashing a quick one-two of daggers at the trio of rata I'd spotted.

One of the daggers found its mark and the rata fell, writhing and squeaking as it fought the inevitable. The second missed.

I hurried forward, magic firing from my hands and zapping the little rodents hard enough to stun them. When I got close, I picked up Milo's fallen blade and drove it into the chest of the next demon. The third made it halfway across the warehouse floor before Milo's magic froze it in place. He stalked over, picked it up, and broke its neck.

I wrinkled my nose. "Gross."

KISS OF DEATH   159

"No judging. I got it done."

He dropped the dead demon and wiped his hands on his pants, his lip curling in disgust.

I retrieved Milo's blades and handed them back to him then pulled out the burner phone Rigo had issued and snapped a pic of the evidence of our hunt. After firing off a text to Rigo, I turned back to where Milo was trying to wipe his blades clean on the fur of the demon at his feet.

"This blood is sticky," he complained.

I opened my mouth to tell him to clean up later, but movement just behind him caught my eye.

My eyes widened.

My jaw dropped.

I struggled to find my voice in time.

"Milo, watch out!"

A wall of pudgy, gray flesh swung out, smacking Milo from behind. He went flying, arms outstretched, before slamming against the far wall. He grunted and then went still.

My chest tightened with worry, but there was no time to check on Milo. Not now.

I looked back at the hulking silhouette that had so rudely intruded on us.

My eyes narrowed as I took in the six-foot tall demon. It had a lumpy torso that reminded me a bit of cotton candy gone moldy and every inch of it was covered in goo.

Yahtzee.

"You snot-nosed little . . ."

I grit my teeth and grabbed for the blade tucked into my boot. It flipped end over end until the tip bounced harmlessly off the demon's skin and only served to make its three eyes narrow in irritation.

Damn.

I'd read about how tough a snorgaut's flesh could be, but I'd never seen it up close. Until now.

Its mouth opened, a gurgly roar building from deep in its throat, and a half-eaten rata demon fell out. The rodent-turned-snack hit the floor with a wet thud. On its heels, slime sprayed from its open maw.

Shit.

I barely made it out of the way.

Lifting my hands, I tried again, this time hitting it with a magic fireball, but the flames barely singed the demon's chin hair before winking out.

The gray snorgaut demon surged toward me, its wide torso stretching across the doorway at its back. I was boxed in and without backup.

Milo still hadn't moved, and I couldn't spare the time to go to him now.

Hopefully, he would recover. And hopefully, someone would come looking for us soon when we didn't show up at the meeting point.

For now, it was up to me to take care of this asshole.

I scrambled to where Milo lay unconscious and

snagged his daggers from the cargo pocket of his pants. With one gripped firmly in each hand, I turned and charged at the snorgaut rushing me.

Slime sprayed from its mouth and nose, and I twisted to avoid getting hit.

At the last second, I leaped, using my momentum to scale the beast and then twist onto its back. With my thighs gripping its neck, I buried each of the daggers in an eyeball.

The demon screamed loud enough to rattle the windows. It twisted violently, tossing me aside. Pain lanced through me as I landed hard on my hip then tucked and let the momentum carry me forward. I rolled and came up on my feet, turning in time to see its meaty hands ripping the blades free, a long, thin trail of slime attached to each tip.

My stomach heaved as I watched more slimy goo leaking from its injured eyes.

The demon moaned then stumbled and fell.

I jumped to my feet and hurried to finish this.

Calling up my shifter magic, I let my beast take shape. Gone were my pointed ears and lean body. By the time I reached the writhing monster, I was half-griffin, with claws where my hands had been and a sharpened beak for a mouth.

Giving in to my beast, I tore the demon's eyes from their sockets then buried the daggers in its heart.

The demon went down easily then.

Panting and utterly grossed out, I backed away, letting

my beast fade. I'd just returned to my fae form when footsteps sounded from the doorway at my back.

I raised my hands, ready with another burst of magic, just as Rigo rushed inside.

"Whoa, it's just me," he called when he saw my ready stance.

Behind him, three more agents spilled into the space. I watched as they assessed the scene and broke off to check on Milo and approach the dead demons.

"Nice timing," I told Rigo.

"Looks like you had more than you bargained for."

Something about his tone had me sharpening my attention.

"Three ratas and a snorgaut demon," I said carefully.

It was more than they'd warned us about. Had he known that snorgaut would be here too? Had he set me up?

"No signs of life among the demons, sir," one of the agents called back.

Rigo nodded. "Call for cleanup. Secure the area until this can be dealt with."

They all exchanged more instructions, but I tuned them out and hurried over to Milo. Professor Thorne was bent over him, fingers searching Milo's throat for a pulse.

My magic hummed, and I used it to probe my friend's life force.

It was there.

Thank the angel.

"He's alive." I sagged against the wall, finally feeling the exhaustion left behind in the wake of the adrenaline I'd been operating on.

"What happened?" Rigo demanded, coming closer.

"The snorgaut got a good hit in," I said without looking up.

"What kind of idiot gets that close to a snorgaut?" Rigo asked.

I shot him a look. "The kind who helped distract it long enough for me to take it down."

Rigo looked ready to argue.

"He's coming around," Professor Thorne said, and Rigo fell silent.

Milo's eyes fluttered.

I bent closer, exhaling in relief as I watched him wake up.

"What happened?" His voice was groggy. "Did we get it?"

"We got it," I assured him. "You did great."

His eyes found mine, and he smiled a wobbly smile. "We make a hell of a team, Hawkins."

"Damn right we do."

"Next time, how about *you* get body-slammed and *I* save the day?"

I grinned and offered my hand to help him up. "Deal. Come on. I'll buy lunch."

FOURTEEN

The next morning, I stood along the outskirts of the group and scanned the faces of those gathered. Tony wasn't among them. He hadn't been at breakfast either.

"Maybe he pissed of Rodrigo and got kitchen duty," Milo said.

"Or maybe he mysteriously turned green and they disappeared him," I muttered.

Milo shot me a look.

It was a terrible joke but only because I was starting to worry the truth wasn't far from it.

Before I could voice my fears, something hit me in the back.

I turned and frowned at the weapon in Faith's hand. The ball on the end of the handle was spiked, and my back was now throbbing because of it.

"What the hell," I grumbled.

"Hey, losers. You're in my way. Move your ass."

Faith smiled sweetly—in a serial killer kind of way.

Milo eyed her. "I don't move for nasty women or trolls. You decide which category you fall into."

Faith's jaw dropped. Her eyes narrowed, but her response was cut short.

"Milo Greene?"

Professor Thorne worked her way through the crowd of students and stopped in front of Milo. Faith stepped back to give the older woman space.

"Ma'am?" Milo said.

"You're to report upstairs for final testing today," Professor Thorne said.

Milo frowned. "Ma'am? I thought finals weren't for another week."

"Finals are administered once the student has shown sufficient aptitude for placement," she said flatly.

"What does that mean?" he asked.

"It means our instructors already have an idea about where to place you," she explained. "Your final exam tells us whether we're right."

"Sounds like you guys should be the ones taking the test if you're so unsure," he joked.

Professor Thorne just stared back at him, clearly unamused.

"Right then. I'll just get going," Milo muttered, shuffling off. He shot a glance at me. "See you at lunch," he mouthed before hurrying out.

"What about me, ma'am?" Faith asked.

"What about you?" Professor Thorne asked.

"Aren't I being called upstairs to test?" she asked. "I took down my mud demon in record time during my field test."

"You mean you and Mr. Trettel took it down."

Faith's smile faltered. "Of course. Anyway, surely you've recognized my aptitude for detective work by now."

Professor Thorne sniffed, gave Faith a once-over that made my day, and walked off without a word.

I wished Milo had stayed long enough to see it.

"You're all here because you've completed your courses," Professor Thorne said to those assembled. "All that's left is your final exam. Starting today, you'll spend your morning in this room, and we'll do all we can to prepare you for the test to come."

"How can we prepare without magic?" someone asked.

She smiled thinly. "Your magic will sharpen you, but you must not rely on it. Prove to me you can do your job without it."

Well, that didn't sound fun.

The next couple of hours were spent running hypothetical drills and being tested on our strategy in the field. None of it was from our textbook, and the longer it went, the more outlandish the setups became. By the time we were wrapping up, I realized this was the real test; running scenarios no one could prepare for or see coming.

Professor Thorne made it clear none of us had all the answers. I just hoped Milo did. And that he aced whatever exam they were giving him.

After lunch, we resumed.

By the end of the day, the exhaustion had taken its toll on everyone. When class ended for the day, we all made our way to the cafeteria in relative silence. Between the pressure to pass and the physical exhaustion, I was done. Even Faith was quiet. Somehow, knowing the Queen B herself had been affected made me feel mildly better.

By dinner, Tony still hadn't shown, and I was beginning to worry.

Dumping my half-eaten tray, I headed for the clinic.

Leslie wasn't at her desk, but I found Starla in the hall. She had shadows under her eyes and a deep-set frown that only lightened a little when she saw me coming.

"Gem, everything okay? Do you need the nurse?"

"I was looking for a friend, actually. Tony Coffell. He wasn't in class or at lunch."

"Of course. He tested out last night and was released for duty."

I stopped short. "What?"

"Professor Garcia observed his final evaluation, and he was assigned according to his performance." She said the words with mounting confusion. "Is there a problem?"

"No, I . . . He didn't tell me his exam was coming up so fast."

"Maybe he didn't know."

I frowned, thinking of the way they'd just sprung it on Milo today. And last night, when we'd returned from our demon test, I'd spent the evening in the clinic with Milo while he recovered. Maybe Tony had come looking and hadn't known where to find us.

"Exams are scheduled based on instructor availability and student readiness. Sometimes that means last-minute scheduling."

"Do you know what the outcome was?" I asked. "Where he was assigned."

"I'm not permitted to give that information out," she said. "Privacy reasons. You understand."

"Of course."

I hesitated.

"Anything else?"

"That's all, thanks."

I made my way back to the dorms, fingers crossed Tony had at least been assigned something local. Hopefully, he'd been given leave and was maybe even now on Fiona's doorstep with a dozen roses. The thought made me smile even if it did make me sad for Milo.

The halls were empty by the time I made my way back to my room. Kicking the door shut behind me, I jumped at the sight of someone stretched out on my bed.

When I saw it was Milo, I relaxed.

"Shit, you scared me." I kicked his feet aside and sat on the mattress beside him. "How'd it go?"

One look at his expression and I knew it wasn't good.

"Toledo," he said flatly.

"What the heck is a Toledo?"

"A city in Ohio, apparently."

"What's important about it?"

"Nothing, at least in my opinion. But it's where I've been cross-assigned."

"Wait, the agency is sending you to Toledo?"

"If I want a patrol job, that's my only option."

"What if you took another job?"

"Rodrigo informed me Burger Bin is hiring."

"Ugh. What a prick." I sat beside Milo, shoulders sagging. "I'm sorry."

"The worst part is I nailed the exam. Took out a wraith demon before it could get out a single moan."

"That's great," I said.

He shook his head. "Didn't matter. It's like they'd already made up their minds."

We sat in silence.

"Tony passed too," I said finally.

Milo looked up. "Where's he assigned?"

"No idea. Starla gave me some line about privacy protocol."

"Everything about this place is stupid."

"Maybe he's in Toledo too."

"God, I hope not. No one deserves that."

"It could be great." I hit his knee. He grunted.

Shoving him aside, I crawled in and laid next to him.

"My dad once told me Ohio has great hot dogs," I said finally.

He shot me a sideways look. "If you make a wiener joke right now, I will punch you in the tit."

"Fine. I'll make it when I come visit you."

He propped his head on his elbow and looked down at me. "Promise?"

"Of course. I bet they have great roads for drag racing since only like three people live there anyway."

He scowled. "Not helping."

I grinned. "Sorry. But seriously, go to Toledo. Kill some demons. Impress the higher-ups. Request a transfer. You'll be back in the French Quarter before you know it."

"They're separating us because we're too much for one city to handle," he said.

"It's a conspiracy," I agreed.

He sighed then dropped a kiss to the tip of my nose. "Fine. I'll go and kick ass. But when I get transferred back here, you're buying dinner."

"All the wieners you can eat."

FIFTEEN

"Gem Hawkins, please report to my office." Starla's voice woke me from a dead sleep. For a terrifying second, I thought she was standing in my dorm room.

My heart raced as I rolled over, looking around wildly. Squinting into the shadowy darkness, I made out the familiar shape of my desk and chair. Other than that, the room was empty.

"Gem Hawkins." Starla's voice was tinny and far away.

I exhaled. "Ugh, what?"

I rubbed my face, hoping to clear my thoughts. The clock beside my bed read three-fourteen.

What the hell?

"Please report to my office immediately."

The loudspeaker crackled then went silent.

Right. She was calling me over the intercom. But what

was urgent enough to make her do it in the middle of the night?

I got dressed quickly, throwing a sweatshirt on over my loose tee, and then padded into the hallway in my socks and sweatpants.

Dim lighting washed everything in yellow-tinged shadows. For the millionth time, I wished my fae magic were available to help me navigate. But as usual, my magic was stripped outside the group training areas. I ran a hand through my bedhead hair and kept going, ears strained for any sign I wasn't alone. If this was some kind of test, some ambush waiting to happen, I wanted to be ready.

But nothing jumped out at me. No sign of instructors lurking or conjured demons blocking my way. At the end of the hall, I turned left and crept past the clinic toward the door I'd come through that first day I'd arrived at the Tiff.

Months ago now. It felt like years.

The door called to me like a siren. On the other side of that was the freedom Tony had talked about. It was dinner with Mom and sandwich tastings with Lila and laughter and sunshine and speed.

It was also a world in which my father's killer currently walked free. If I left now, whoever had threatened me would win.

I turned away from the door, knocking on Starla's office instead.

"Come in."

Pushing the door open, I blinked at the bright light. Starla sat behind a polished desk, her hair and makeup flawless despite the time of night.

"You wanted to see me," I said.

She gestured to the chairs. "Sit. We need to chat."

I dropped into one of the chairs, panic spiking at her serious tone.

"Is everything okay?" I asked. "Is it my mother?"

"Your mother?" She frowned. "I have no idea. No, this is about you, Gem."

"Me?"

"I've been watching your performance here over these last weeks, and I think you're a great asset to wherever you'll land when you've finished your training."

"Okay." I still didn't understand where this was going or why it had to be said at three in the morning.

"I'd like it if you landed here. With me."

"Like an instructor position?"

"Not quite. You'd be assisting me directly."

Either I was exhausted and not understanding her right or she'd just asked me to be her secretary.

"And what position is that, exactly?"

Even after weeks and weeks under the same roof, I still had no idea what Starla actually did.

"I'm looking for a set of eyes and ears. You've become friends with, not just the recruits, but some of our staff as well."

"I'm just being nice," I said carefully.

"And you notice more than you let on."

"I'm not sure what you're getting at."

She smiled tightly. "What can you tell me about Leslie?"

"The nurse?" I frowned. "She's . . . capable? And nice."

"Capable and nice." Starla folded her hands on the desk. "That's your professional assessment? As a detective, I mean."

"I wasn't aware I should be using my detective skills on the staff."

"A good detective should always be assessing everyone, don't you think?"

What the hell was this? Some kind of test?

Fine.

"Leslie is pleasant but gullible. She's not very observant and a terrible liar."

Starla's lips twitched. "Tell me more."

I kept my gaze even and my face carefully blank. Where was this all going?

"She's a great asset on your front end. Greeting new recruits, making them feel at home. She makes them believe they're capable of retaining some of the secrecy of their old lives."

"What kind of secrets?" she asked, and my stomach tightened at the knowing look she wore.

"Anything they've managed to skim under the radar of

the hiring teams. She's also friendly enough to feel like a confidante when some of the trainees might need to feel less alone during this process. But—"

I stopped, unsure how honest to be.

"Go on."

Screw it. I was all in.

"The flip side is that your first line of defense against a threat is a creature not equipped to spot them. It wouldn't be difficult for a rebel to sneak through and into the program. Not with Leslie as your gatekeeper."

Starla's eyes glittered. "Insightful. Thorough. What can you tell me about how you came to this conclusion?"

"The lying?" I shrugged. "I don't believe for a second that Desmond Ayers just went home to recover from a flu. There's a cover-up, and one conversation with Leslie gave it away."

"But your fae magic allowed you to read her, I'm sure."

"My magic is stripped," I pointed out. "This had nothing to do with fae senses."

"I see. And the rest? Her gullibility and making recruits believe they retain their secrets...?"

My pulse sped.

"I'd rather not share until I can prove my theories that led to this assessment."

Starla tipped her head back and laughed.

"You're perfect for this."

I frowned. "I'm still not sure what the job is."

"You're doing it now. Assessing our potential weaknesses. Using your detective skills to see what others can't. You've also managed to hang onto your own secrets all the way through the program. A skill most recruits lose around the fourteen-day mark, statistically speaking."

My palms went clammy.

"I'm not sure what you mean."

"Gem, we both know you're capable of shifting into a lot more than just your father's griffin."

My mouth went dry.

"I don't know what you're talking about."

"You do. But you'll die before admitting it. I appreciate that. I need that kind of resolve in an apprentice." Her smile dimmed. Her eyes sharpened. Even without magic, her inner feline seemed to stir. "Discretion and deception. Those are my requirements. And absolute loyalty, of course."

Starla fell silent, waiting. Watching.

"You want a spy," I realized. "Not for the SSF. For you."

"As I said before, you're perceptive. It's one of the reasons I chose you."

"This is why you called me here in the middle of the night. So no one else will know about this."

"Even Leslie's ignorance has its limits."

I hesitated, a refusal on the tip of my tongue. I was here for my own purpose, not to become a spy and errand girl to the Tiff's receptionist. But then if Starla were just a receptionist, she wouldn't need a spy.

"Who do you want me to watch?" I asked.

"Everyone," she said. "But specifically, your instructors. At least to start."

I narrowed my eyes. "Is this about sexual harassment? Because you don't need an inside man to know Rigo's a piece of—"

"This isn't about Rodrigo's penchant for the female recruits."

"So you already know he's a sleaze?"

Starla didn't flinch. "I know a great many things about this place. Including the fact that you have a cell phone stowed underneath your mattress. And that you smuggled an inter-agency memo into the magic-friendly areas to try and decipher the redacted portions. Not to mention you befriended Ollie, which is no small thing."

My jaw dropped a little, and I glanced around the office. Were there cameras somewhere I hadn't seen?

Part of me wanted to ask if she knew Milo had actually gotten his hands on a deciphered version of the report—or if she knew about the favor he'd traded to get it.

"I know you think I don't do much here, but that's not an accident. It's imperative the recruits—and the instructors, for that matter—continue to underestimate me."

"Who do you report to?" I asked, trying to put all the pieces together about what Starla's job really was.

"No one you should concern yourself with," she said, and I knew she had no intention of giving me names. Not tonight, anyway. "If you agree to do this, you will report directly to me and no one else. If you prove useful, and we both survive the next few months, then we can talk about introductions."

If we survive?

"And if I don't agree?" I asked.

Would she give up my secret? Tell the SSF about my shapeshifting abilities?

She shrugged. "Then we will part ways, and this will have been nothing more than a strange sort of sleepwalk."

I stared at her as the truth behind her words sunk in. "You'd wipe my memory."

She didn't respond.

"But only Nephilim can do that."

More silence.

It didn't matter. She'd just answered my question. Starla reported directly to a Nephilim. I didn't know which one. Or why. That could come later. For now, I had to seize the opportunity in front of me. Spying for a Nephilim was dangerous. It's not like I could trust them or even begin to understand their agenda here. But I couldn't deny the access it might offer.

"All right," I said finally. "But first I need to know you aren't bluffing. That you have information others don't."

"What would you like to know?"

"Desmond Ayers. What really happened to him?"

"He was infected with some kind of demon disease we've never seen before. He was taken to quarantine at headquarters for more tests and hopefully a cure."

"What kind of disease?"

"If we knew that, he'd already be cured."

I blew out a breath. She hadn't mentioned the undocumented demon issue, but she'd been honest about his condition at least.

"One more question. Where did Tony Coffell get assigned?"

"Tony is working security at headquarters. He's on day shift and has already been spotted with Fiona Davis three nights this week at various restaurants in the city."

My body relaxed in silent relief. Tony was okay.

A beat of silence passed between us while I thought about everything Starla was offering—and asking of me.

"All right," I said finally.

Starla leaned forward. "Does this mean we have a deal?"

"Yeah," I said, hoping I wasn't making the biggest mistake ever. "I'll spy for you."

SIXTEEN

A fennec demon lay dead at my feet, its thick goo coating my face and hands. I opened my mouth to suck in a breath and with it came the bitter taste of slime against my tongue. My stomach rolled. I gagged, and my beast took over until I'd shifted to my griffin form without conscious thought.

Somewhere in the training area, a scream sounded. My griffin's head whipped around, shifting as I turned. The training arena became more and more empty with each passing day. Three quarters of my class had already tested out, which meant more room to move around during these practice trials. It also meant more demons per recruit to take down since Rigo didn't believe in proper ratios between agents and monsters.

This far into the session, most of the demons had already fallen, but several had also been lit on fire. Probably courtesy of Langdon, the warlock with ink-stained hands. He'd gotten pretty good at conjuring fireballs lately.

I squinted through the smoky haze, my griffin fading as I realized the worst of the danger had passed. By the time I spotted the source of the screams, I was back on two legs, every inch of me still coated in goo.

"Back up," Faith yelled, and I realized she was the source of the panic.

An arachnid demon had cornered her against a brick wall. The building at her back had been spelled to look like a daycare full of human children. One of the demon's back legs shot out, slicing at Faith's already-bloody arms. At the same time, Faith swung out with a long-handled blade, its sharp end aimed at the demon's throat. She faltered when the demon's leg made contact.

On a sharp noise of pain, Faith's body listed sideways and pain contorted her features.

I stepped over the pile of goo and guts that had been a demon up until ten seconds ago, then sprinted for Faith.

Flinging magic ahead of me, I watched as the force of my fae power shuddered through the arachnid demon, temporarily stunning it. I wasn't capable of anything lethal with those blasts, but I'd learned how to sharpen what I had into something pretty damn painful. I knew because Rigo had made us shoot ourselves with our own magic three weeks ago just to see what it felt like. Three different warlocks had wet themselves from their self-inflicted pain. Langdon Potts had nearly burned to death.

With the arachnid demon stunned, Faith slid her blade into the demon's head, killing it with one blow.

I watched as the demon fell in a tangle of limbs.

Faith looked up, and our eyes locked.

"Thanks," she said, breathless and glassy-eyed.

"Don't mention it."

"I probably won't," she admitted, her face pale and coated in a sheen of sweat.

Then she was out of my line of sight as two of the medics rushed over to inspect her wounds. Already, Faith's lacerations were oozing with the demon spider's poison. After an urgent round of questions from the medics, Faith was rushed from the room.

Finally, I turned to survey the damage we'd done with our kills.

One of the far walls was crumbling where another demon had smashed into it in an attempt to crush a recruit. The training room floor was made up of several dozen dead demons and their ever-widening puddle of poisons and goo. But all of that would be cleaned up and re-glamoured before next time. What I cared about most were the recruits. At a glance, everyone else looked relatively unharmed.

"Weapons down," Professor Thorne called. "Please assemble in the center for debrief."

Slowly, I made my way over piles of rubble and guts. A few disgusted glances were thrown my way as my classmates noticed how much goo I'd been coated in. No one walked too close as we all reassembled in the center for debriefing.

"You okay?" Cliff asked.

"Yeah, I look worse than I feel," I told him.

"Nah." He grinned. "You wear it well."

I ignored his flirty tone, but he didn't seem to mind. Cliff's interest had moved into a comfortable space. Like he knew it was never going anywhere and didn't seem to mind too much. He'd started following Violet around instead.

"Hawkins!"

Rigo marched up, his face flushed.

"What the hell was that stunt?" he demanded.

I frowned in confusion. "Demon slaying?"

"Try again."

"*Messy* demon slaying?"

Cliff snickered.

"We have a strict rule against assisting other recruits unless otherwise partnered up. Or did you forget?"

"You mean Faith?" I glanced at the still-twitching arachnid demon. "You gave her a level three. The thing had already broken her skin and was poisoning her. You can't expect me to stand by and just watch it happen."

"I can, and I did. You failed this assignment. Your final

exam is suspended effective immediately. I'll let you know when and if I reschedule it."

"Wait, you can't just pull my final. I'm due to test out this week."

He glared at me, rage dancing behind his dark eyes. "Don't you dare tell me what I can and can't do. I'm in charge here. Not you."

"Well then maybe you should act like it," I hissed.

His eyes went wide, and I knew I'd gone too far.

I'd just talked back to an instructor, which was a big no-no. And to top it off, there were witnesses to back it up.

I was screwed.

Out of the corner of my eye, I saw Professor Thorne wedging past the others. In about three seconds, I was going to be in serious trouble for insubordination. But dammit, what did they expect? I wasn't going to let them punish me for not letting Faith die. Even I didn't dislike her that much.

"What's happening here?" Professor Thorne demanded.

Rigo continued to stare me down, but I forced my gaze to hers. "Nothing, ma'am. Instructor Garcia was reminding me of the rules."

My tone was stiff, but at least I'd said the right words.

"And you'll do well to remember them," she said. "Now, hit the showers. You smell disgusting."

"Yes, ma'am." I nodded and started for the locker room,

already strategizing about how to go around Rigo to resolve this.

"A shower isn't going to be enough to remove that stick up her ass," Rigo muttered. "Hell, even her father's death couldn't do it."

The words were so soft, I wouldn't have heard them without my fae senses. But I wasn't the only one with super-hearing.

A few gasps sounded.

Rage crept through me, and my inner beast snarled. Suddenly, every unshed tear and unspoken slice of rage I'd harbored for an unnamed killer wanted out. And it wanted me to unleash it on Rigo Garcia.

I whirled and closed the distance, my fist connecting with Rigo's face before he or anyone else could move a muscle.

The crack sounded loudly against the shocked silence.

Rigo buckled, nearly losing his balance before catching himself. Straightening, he held a hand to his eye, using the other to glare back at me. Then he started forward in response, and I braced myself, hands fisted, while I waited for him to come.

Professor Thorne stepped between us, driving Rigo back with obvious effort.

He growled at her attempt to stop him and nearly yanked free when she muttered a few quiet words and

Rigo's feet went still. He strained against her magic but nothing he tried unstuck him.

Professor Thorne turned to face me, eyes blazing. "Don't even think about it, recruit."

"He can't talk about my father like that."

"I agree," Professor Thorne said.

I blinked at her, surprised into stillness. "You do?"

"Of course I do. That was a terrible thing to say." Her expression turned to a warning. "But you shouldn't have hit him."

"The bitch assaulted me," Rigo yelled.

The training doors opened. Kinrade and Wayne walked in. When they saw the three of us facing off, and Rigo still struggling to get free from Thorne's spell, they increased their pace.

"What's going on here?" Starla asked, rushing in behind them.

"That's better explained elsewhere," Professor Thorne said before Rigo could say a word. She gave a pointed chin-nod toward the other recruits. "Miranda, why don't you take care of them and we'll all meet in my office?"

Professor Kinrade nodded and hurried toward the remaining recruits, ushering them toward the locker rooms.

"Time to shower and get to your next class," she told them as the crowd scattered. Cliff gave me a look and then reluctantly followed the others.

"Follow me," Professor Thorne said and started for the rear exit; a door that led to staff quarters.

I followed her, and Starla fell in behind me.

"What about me?" Rigo demanded.

Without turning, Professor Thorne raised her hand above her head and snapped her fingers. Rigo's answering grunt was proof he'd just been unstuck.

Ten minutes later, all four instructors and Starla were all staring back at me as I finished telling my side of what had happened starting with Faith nearly getting killed and ending with Rigo getting sucker punched.

"She's broken too many rules," Rigo said when I was done. "Expulsion is the only obvious choice here."

"You talked shit about her dead father," Professor Wayne said.

I shot him a grateful glance, but when my eyes landed on his Hawaiian shirt, I looked away. Milo had officially made it weird.

"She assaulted me," Rigo said emphatically. "And don't forget about how she helped another recruit during a solo test."

"Yes, let's talk about that," Starla said, crossing her arms as she looked at Rigo. "So, you were aware Faith Burkhart was mortally wounded and you hadn't intervened?"

Rigo scowled. "I had it under control."

"Yeah, it sounds like it," Starla said dryly.

"It was a teaching moment," he shot back.

"Mmm-hmm."

"At any rate, it is against policy for recruits to physically assault instructors," Professor Thorne said, and I tensed.

Shit.

For all this hard work to be ruined because Rigo had goaded me into kicking his ass . . . I didn't even want to think about how mad I'd be at myself for this when I had to go back to work at Lila's Sandwich Shop after all this.

"She was baited," Starla said. "I hardly think we can blame her for reacting."

Rigo's eyes widened. "Who's side are you on?" he demanded.

Starla's gaze hardened. "I'm on the side of the SSF, Rigo. What about you?"

"What the hell kind of question is that? Of course I'm loyal to the agency."

"Then you'll see the wisdom in my idea," Starla said. Turning to Professor Thorne and the other instructors, she added, "I think I have a solution that will benefit all parties here."

"What do you have in mind?" Professor Thorne asked.

"In three days, there's a ball," Starla began.

Instructor Kinrade's eyes widened. "You don't mean The Monster Ball?"

Starla offered a small smile. "I do, in fact. And I happen to have an invite."

"What does The Monster Ball have to do with Rigo getting punched?" Professor Thorne asked.

Starla hesitated then turned to me. "Gem, be a dear and wait outside for a moment, would you?"

"Sure." I slipped past them to the door, ignoring Rigo's protests.

In the hall, I strained to hear the conversation going on without me, but the moment the door had shut, I felt the veil slip into place. They were purposely shutting me out.

I hovered in the hall, still covered in goo and too nervous to move a single step away. The fact that I hadn't been expelled yet gave me a small bit of hope. And if Starla was going to bat for me, no matter how weird her idea sounded so far, that had to count for something.

Now, more than ever, I was glad I'd accepted her job offer. It was probably the only thing keeping me here. But a ball? How did a fancy party solve my problem and keep me from getting fired?

A few minutes later, the door reopened and Professor Thorne motioned for me to reenter. Inside the small office, Rigo's face was flushed bright red, except for his eye, which was swollen and already turning purple.

It was my favorite look on him to date.

The others looked mildly unsure about whatever they'd discussed and were giving me a once-over like they'd never seen me before. I tried to keep my chin high, hoping I would pass their inspection. Being covered in demon guts probably didn't help my case. As proof, Instructor Kinrade wrinkled her nose when I got close.

"Gem, you violated one of our most important rules today," Professor Thorne began, and my stomach dropped. "Physically assaulting an instructor is grounds for immediate termination from the program."

I tried to acknowledge her words around the lump in my throat. "I understand."

"However," she said, and I looked up sharply. "Starla has brought an interesting proposition to our attention. An opportunity that serves two purposes. First, it gives us a shot to make contact with a high-profile target toward an outcome that would impact every species of supes on this planet."

Every species? Wow. Okay, no pressure.

"And two, it would allow you one more shot at taking your final exam after all."

I stared at her, surprise and gratitude overwhelming me. "Thank you."

"You understand that by all counts, you should be expelled at this very moment. This is a second chance. The only one you'll get."

"Yes, and I appreciate it more than you know."

Rigo grumbled something about everyone working against him.

"The only reason we're allowing you the opportunity to test at all is the fact that we can send you into the field to do so."

"The field?" I repeated, confused. Weren't all finals performed in the real world?

"Yes. In three days, you'll be briefed and sent to a party called The Monster Ball."

"What's that?" I asked.

"An annual gala thrown by supernaturals," Starla explained.

"It's all the who's who of the supe world," Professor Kinrade added in a hushed voice.

"Have you ever been?" I asked.

"No," she said, eyeing me with a twinge of jealousy.

"And where is this party held exactly?" I asked.

"No one knows. The party location changes yearly. Even the identity of the proprietor is a mystery."

"Then how do we know I can get in?" I asked.

Professor Thorne motioned at Rigo. "Give her the invitation."

Rigo grudgingly handed me the slip of paper he'd been holding. I read it quickly then looked back at Professor Thorne and the others.

"I still don't understand how I get there."

"For security purposes, we can't explain just yet," Professor Thorne said. "You'll be briefed when the time comes. And then you'll attend the ball. If you're successful at your task, you'll pass the program and graduate. If you fail, you'll be sent home. Do you understand?"

"Yes, ma'am. And thank you."

"Don't thank me yet." She hesitated. "Rigo will run the mission from here. He's your point of contact. Your *only* point of contact."

I tried not to let my displeasure show at her words. Of course it would be Rigo. The one person in this room who actually wanted me to fail.

"And you'll be flying solo," she went on. "That ticket admits only one, which means no one from the Tiff can accompany you as backup. Whatever happens, you're on your own. Do you have any questions for me about this?"

Now I understood about sending me into the field.

"No. I'll be ready."

Professor Thorne nodded. "You're dismissed."

"Thank you," I told her again. "Thank you all. I won't let you down."

Professor Thorne waved me off. "Wonderful. And for the angel's sake, take a shower."

SEVENTEEN

"Gemini Hawkins, please report to the staging area for briefing."

The voice over the loudspeaker echoed throughout the building—and inside every cell of my body. When the announcement was finished, I shared a tight smile with Starla, my wardrobe consultant for tonight.

We'd met twice since our first meeting. Both times so I could give her my thoughts on the instructors I'd met here. I had no clue what she was looking for, and I hadn't offered anything earth-shattering, but both times Starla had nodded and taken down notes like I'd just cracked the case on something big.

She hadn't spoken to me outside the secret briefings, but I could see the change in the way she watched me. Like we had a secret. Or like maybe she was trying to spot my weaknesses in case I failed to keep that secret.

Milo would have loved it, but with him and the others gone, I was itching to ace tonight's final and get the hell out of the Tiff for good. Though I wasn't sure where that would leave Starla and I.

"Gem, you're ready," she assured me now. "That dress is stunning."

"Thank you," I told her despite the nerves dancing in my belly.

She tossed her brown waves off her shoulder. "The red gets them every time, you know. All eyes are going to be on you."

I frowned. "Is that a good idea? I mean, wouldn't it be smarter to blend in so I don't get noticed?"

Starla shook her head, a small smile on her pale pink lips. "Gem, you will never blend in. You're too beautiful to go unnoticed, red dress or not. Best to embrace your strengths rather than downplay them."

"I guess that makes sense."

Or I could shapeshift into something ugly. Like Ollie.

Starla ran a hand lightly over my white-blonde hair, smoothing it back where she'd done it up into an intricate twist. A few loose strands framed my face, and she tucked one of them away again as she said, "The trick is to let them see only what you want them to. Make them watch your right hand, and they'll never suspect what you've done with your left. Understand?"

"Yes."

"Good." She patted my cheek just hard enough to set my teeth on edge. Then she ushered me toward the door. "Go get 'em, darling. When you return, you and I will have a chat about what comes next."

If I returned. But I didn't want to think about that.

With a quick thanks, I hurried out, stopping in my room long enough to grab the single item I knew I'd be expected to bring to my briefing: my invitation to tonight's ball. Then I made my way down the hall as fast as my skinny heels would allow.

The moment I stepped into the training room, my magic returned and my nerves kicked into high gear.

It didn't matter how many training ops I aced, or hell, races I won, I still got nervous as hell before a mission. Tonight was no exception. In fact, dressed up in this monkey suit was making it worse. I hated heels. The trade-off was that I didn't have to even try to appear human tonight.

In answer, the beast inside me reared up. Even with nearly any form available to me, there was only one that had a mind of its own. My griffin's need for a fight nearly knocked me over. Apparently, I'd left him caged too long.

Forcing my beast to calm, I paused long enough to brace a hand against the wall and suck in a few large gulps of air before continuing on. The sliver of parchment clutched in my sweaty hand was going to disintegrate if I didn't get my shit together.

But it was hard to forget how much was riding on tonight.

Being a recruit wasn't my future. Being a detective assigned to top cases was. Tonight was the final step toward making that future a present. And if the looks I'd gotten from the recruits I'd passed in the hall were any indication, I was going to look damn good doing it.

As if to drive the point home, I rounded the corner onto the platform that led into our staging area, and Rigo's eyes practically fell out of his head. He stood on the ground floor next to a glass counter lit by LEDs all the way around. The entire room was done that way. It would have been fancy and beautiful in an art gallery but—oh, who was I kidding? It was fancy and beautiful now, the way it lit up all the gleaming black guns and shiny silver knives mounted to the walls.

Rigo watched as I made my way down the single flight of stairs and across the gleaming white floor to where he stood. He wore his usual uniform: black pants and a black shirt paired with black steel-toed boots. He thought it made him look tougher. I thought it made him look like a goth who hadn't matured past seventh grade sex-ed.

At least his black eye hadn't completely healed.

I bit back a smirk as I studied the damage my fist had done.

"Damn girl." He licked his lips, making no effort to hide his visual perusal. "You look..."

"Mission ready?" I offered, my eyes narrowing. I would have crossed my arms over my chest, but considering the push-up effect it would have on my already-exposed cleavage, I decided against it.

At my words, Rigo dialed back the panting. His eyes still gleamed with thinly veiled desire, but he nodded.

"Starla's got a great eye," he agreed, and I could all but see the drool he was holding back.

"Is everything ready?"

He nodded, picking up a tiny black object from the counter in front of him. He offered it to me, and I strode forward to take it, my red heels clicking over the floor. Rigo's gaze wandered over my bare legs and then back up again as I grabbed the comm unit and slid it into my ear.

Once in place, I clicked the button to activate the two-way speaker system—and the cloaking magic that would render the tiny thing invisible in my pointed fae ears.

"Test, test," I said.

"Loud and clear," he answered.

I pretended not to notice the smell of cologne splashed over cigarette smoke.

"Here. Take this." He handed me a small silver clutch with glittering embellishments. I opened it and frowned at the contents. Lip gloss and a small cell phone.

I looked up at Rigo. "No weapons?"

"You can't carry inside the party. It's rule number one for attending."

"Then how am I supposed to—"

"Not every mission will allow for weapons, Hawkins. That was part of your training. Now, you'll have your comm unit, a cell phone which has my number already programmed, and you'll have this." He reached into my clutch and pulled out the lip gloss.

I watched as he yanked the cap free and gave the tube a half-twist. "If you get into real trouble, twist this all the way up and it'll emit a laughing gas. It won't last long, but it'll give you a chance to make an exit if you need it."

"Laughing gas?" My brows shot up. "Really? That's the best you can do?"

He shrugged and recapped the gloss before dropping it into my purse. "Be glad you got that. Weapons are impossible to smuggle in."

I arched a brow. Rigo wasn't usually the type to play by someone else's rules. "Security's that tight?"

He shook his head. "There's no security. Well, none you can see anyway."

"Then why—"

"Because the magic that goes into this party is like nothing you've ever seen. The spell work will have the place locked down, so don't even think about trying to get through it."

"I'm sure I can handle it," I began, but he just huffed at me.

"That's not the mission," he snapped. "And arguing

will only lose you points. Something you can't afford at this stage, or do I need to remind you what's at stake tonight, recruit?"

Recruit.

He was reminding me where I stood. Or more importantly what I stood to lose.

Asshole.

"No reminder necessary," I said through closed teeth. I was already on thin ice—as he was so quick to point out. Tonight had to make up for all that. Not make it worse. "What's the mission?"

"First, show me your ticket."

I bit back a sarcastic retort about showing mine if he showed his. Rigo would have taken me literally, and then I would have no choice but to punch him.

Again.

He was right. The stakes were high enough already.

Instead, I held up the parchment paper still clutched in my hand. Although, it wasn't really mine per se. It had been *procured* through the proper channels. I had my mark to thank for that, and from the little I'd been told already, I knew he'd expect me to very thankful.

This mission was going to suck ass.

But it was also going to show my superiors what I was capable of. And when it was over and I was no longer Rigo's trainee, I was definitely punching him again.

Rigo eyed the parchment shrewdly then nodded once.

"Good. You'll need that in your hand if you want the magic to deliver you on time."

"Deliver me how?"

"When we're finished here, you'll stand outside in the moonlight." He shrugged as if that explained everything. "From there, the magic does the rest."

"What's the rest?" I asked.

He went on like I hadn't even spoken. "You'll show your ticket at the door. When you're inside, I advise that you go directly to the main ballroom and stay there until you find your mark."

I shook my head, confused. "I thought the ballroom was the only place to go?"

Rodrigo chuckled. "Oh, there are other places to go. Anywhere in the building is fair game, really. The proprietor leaves plenty of dimly lit passageways open for wandering. Bedrooms will be first come first served, and if you find yourself in one of those with a willing partner... Well, let's just say what happens at the ball stays at the ball."

I made a face at the unwanted mental images that came with realizing how Rigo knew so much. "Okay, okay. Point taken. I'll be sure to stick to the ballroom."

"Good." He picked up a tablet lying on the counter and hit a button, illuminating the screen.

A video of a man with dark hair and a slippery smile stared back at me. The audio had been muted, but I didn't need to hear what he was saying to know he was in love with the sound of his own voice. A girl could read these things.

"This is the mark?" I asked.

Rigo nodded. "Kristoff Rasmussen, CEO of Tech Empire Industries."

"He looks like a douchebag," I said, noting the way he'd paused long enough to wink at a female reporter trying to ask a question.

"Well, that douchebag is in possession of a data chip that, if it goes public, could single-handedly expose every single supernatural on the planet."

"I read about this guy," I said, remembering the articles I'd seen recently. "The chip is designed to protect supes from detection so they can fly under the radar in whatever role or job they play in the human world."

"That was its initial purpose, yes, but Rasmussen has reverse-engineered the code and is auctioning it to the highest bidder."

"Reverse-engineered..." I stared at Rigo as the full weight of his implication washed over me. "Meaning it would out every single supe in the world."

Rigo's expression was grim. "Your orders are to recover the chip and deliver it to me without exposing yourself to the mark. He is not to be harmed or tipped off in any way. Am I clear?"

I nodded.

I couldn't believe they were offering a mission so important to a recruit. But then I remembered my cover— and realized the likely reason for sending me was that no one higher up wanted this gig. Or no one wanted to do what it would take to succeed.

It was the perfect assignment for a girl on the brink of expulsion.

"My cover story is that I'm his date-for-hire," I said flatly. This was the only real detail I'd been briefed on and even that had only been disclosed because of the fuss I'd made over the dress Starla had chosen.

"We infiltrated the escort service and replaced their catalog with one of ours." He said it so casually, like one might order a pizza, but my stomach clenched at the use of the word "catalog" as it related to women. "He browsed the options and requested you."

"Lucky me," I muttered.

Rigo's gaze narrowed. "It is *very* lucky," he said. "Considering how badly you need a win, I'd say it's the best luck you've had in months. Complete the mission and you earn your graduation. Fail and... Well, I don't think I have to tell you what will happen if you fail."

I shuddered, and Rigo's lips curved subtly. Asshole was enjoying this.

"I'll complete the mission," I said.

"Good girl." He set the tablet aside, powering it off again. "Let's get you outside."

With my purse in one hand and invitation in the other, I followed him out the side door and through the exit that led to the rooftop track where we ran three mornings a week. Rigo led the way, cutting a path across the grass. He stopped when we reached the track, now empty of recruits, even the hard-core ones like Faith who worked out when we weren't forced to.

Those freaks were weird to me.

"Where's the car?" I asked.

"No car." Rodrigo kept walking, and I opened my mouth then closed it again.

"Then how am I—"

"Didn't you read the invitation?"

I turned it over in my hand, scanning the scrawled words on the back. I had read them, but I'd forgotten. Or, more accurately, I hadn't understood their meaning.

"Just as the moon brought me to you, so shall the moon bring you to the ball," I read. Then I looked up at the back of Rodrigo's head. I'd been handed the invite by Rodrigo himself less than twenty-four hours ago, so unless moonlight was his middle name, I was lost.

"What does it mean?" I asked.

"It means we need you standing in the moonlight, that's what." Rodrigo cast a glance up at the moon that hung low and white in the sky then back to where I'd come to a stop at the edge of the track. He reached for my arm, but I yanked it back.

"Don't touch me," I warned.

"Just stand over there," he said, but I caught him patting his swollen eye when he turned away.

I shuffled sideways then stopped when I reached the beam of moonlight that stretched across the lawn. "Here?"

"Perfect," Rodrigo said.

"What happens next—"

A bright light flashed, like a camera going off, and I threw my hand up to shield my eyes. The air around me changed as the humidity of Louisiana dropped away. Cool, fresh air prickled at my skin, and I pried my eyes open to investigate.

"Rigo, what the hell," I began, blinking furiously to clear the flashes of light from my vision.

There was no answer.

By the time I could see again, Rigo was gone. So was the track and the training building behind that. In its place was a rolling lawn, perfectly manicured complete with vibrant green hedges. I whirled and then stopped to take it all in. Behind me, practically glowing underneath the moonlight, stood a crumbling, abandoned castle. The walls shimmered at the edges thanks to my fae sight; a glamour. I had a feeling it wouldn't look nearly so crumbly—or abandoned—once I was inside.

The fact that I was somewhere far beyond the confining walls of the Tiff wasn't lost. For a long moment, I just stood and took it all in. Not just the castle before me but the sense of freedom. No SSF. No demons to slay. No vendetta to fulfill. Just this moment. Me in the moonlight and the possibilities that awaited.

Reality crept back in far too quickly.

"Hawkins, you copy?"

Rigo's voice in my ear set my teeth on edge.

"I copy."

"Safe landing?"

"All good," I said.

"Get going. Report back when you're inside."

Not bothering to answer, I looked up and breathed the fresh air as I contemplated the night sky. Directly overhead, the moon seemed to wink back at me, beckoning me forward. Ahead, the sprawling castle practically whispered for me to step inside. On a deep breath, I began walking toward it, falling into line behind other arrivals. I was here, and it was time to attend my first ever Monster Ball.

EIGHTEEN

Magic pricked at me as I passed underneath a stone archway that led into a small courtyard. By the time both my feet had crossed the threshold, the sight before me had completely transformed. The castle's crumbling, faded façade was replaced with smooth gray stone that rose at least four stories high. All around the courtyard, fog blanketed the ground, giving the illusion that every guest floated rather than walked toward the veranda just ahead. From inside the curling fog, purple lights twinkled back at me.

A perfect blend of festive and creepy.

Still, I couldn't help the awe that struck me as I swept my gaze over the massive beauty of the place. It even had turrets.

Turrets!

Who the fuck lived in a castle with turrets anymore...

No, this didn't belong to the host. Hostess? Proprietor, that was it. If I remembered Starla's explanation correctly, the party's location changed every year, each time at a borrowed location. Still, who did the scouting for this kind of thing?

I wanted that job.

Demon balls, Milo would eat this shit up.

Maybe when this was all over and I'd done what I set out to do, I'd see how one went about applying to scout locations for the most sought-after event of the year. It didn't sound like a bad retirement plan. Maybe Milo and I could go into business together.

I fell in behind a couple who stood before the massive front doors.

The guy reached into his pocket and withdrew two invitations, his mouth drawn tight while he waited for the bouncer to inspect and approve his ticket. He was handsome with a dangerous edge, but the way he stood looking down at nearly everyone made me wonder if he was more than just a socialite. His posture spoke of royalty.

The woman beside him looked gorgeous in her gossamer gown, its leafy embellishments the only thing standing between admiring eyes and all her important bits.

I gave her points for confidence. Not that she had anything to worry about, from what I could see.

Our eyes met, and she smiled at me.

I smiled back just before her date took her arm and led her inside.

When it was my turn, I climbed the two short steps to the landing and handed my ticket to the bouncer standing before me. Awareness shot through me, and I gasped softly. This guy wasn't just any bouncer. He was a gargoyle. A species that only existed in fairy tales back home.

As if he could sense my shock, he winked.

"Welcome to The Monster Ball," he said in a gravelly voice and waved me toward the open doorway behind him. A soft blue light shone through the archway, beckoning me inside.

"Thank you," I murmured and walked through.

The farther I walked, the dimmer the light became until it vanished altogether, leaving me in utter blackness. I reached for my comm unit, about to call for Rodrigo to tell me what the hell to do next, but then music filled the silence with a sudden crash. Loud and rhythmic and already in full swing, it rattled my bones, almost as if someone had flipped a switch mid-song. I took a step, following the sounds.

A second later, light filtered in once again, and I found myself suddenly standing in a large ballroom complete with a stage. Above the platform, a spotlight shone directly over the band currently rocking out.

On the front of the drums, the band's name hung on a neon purple sign that read "Dastardly Deeds."

I did a full spin, then another, trying to take it all in at once. The room was huge, bigger than anywhere else I'd ever seen, and dripping with expensive décor. Two rows of chandeliers ran the length of the rectangular room, all of them lit with twinkling lights that didn't offer much more than multicolored mood lighting in the otherwise dimly lit space.

Curious, I squinted up at the chandelier above me and spotted tiny pixies dancing inside each of the globes. Pixie lights. Clever.

And fancy.

Pixies labor wasn't cheap.

But then my gaze caught on the rest of the décor hanging from the ceiling and all I could do was stare, open-mouthed.

Mattresses. Suspended from the ceiling. And it wasn't hard to figure out what they were intended for, considering one of them was already being put to use by not two but three distinct silhouettes. The shadows made it impossible to make out anything specific and the music way too loud to hear anything going on up there—and that was fine by me.

I glanced down again and noted the fog smoke curling around my feet just like it had outside. So much for impressing them with my fancy heels.

"Crazy, isn't it?"

The voice was so close, I nearly yelped. When I looked up,

an indigo-eyed fairy smiled sympathetically at me. The glitter dusting her nose and cheeks sparkled underneath the lights, and her smile was open, friendly. "First time?" she asked.

I winced. "Am I that obvious?"

She laughed; a delicate tinkling sound that reminded me of wind chimes. "Come on. I'll buy you a drink. Alcohol makes it easier to take it all in."

I spun and followed her to the bar behind me. I hadn't even noticed it before, gawking in only one direction and all. But now, I couldn't miss it. A long bar ran the entire length of this half of the room. Behind it, stood a female bartender with red eyes and ghostly white hair. Her leather bustier left almost nothing to the imagination, and even I couldn't help the attraction or the urge to walk over and run my hand along her curvy torso.

I blinked, trying to clear my head, as I realized her pull on me probably wasn't just chemical.

"Damned succubus," I muttered.

They, too, were supposedly extinct. Especially considering the SSF had once labeled them demon offspring and tried purging them all. Better I didn't out myself as an agent at a party like this one.

As if she could read my mind, she looked right at me and smiled. "What'll it be, love?"

"She'll have a Party In Your Mouth," said my new friend.

I shot her a horrified look, and my jaw fell open a little at the obvious innuendo. "What? No, I..." I looked help- lessly at the smiling succubus.

They both laughed.

"Relax, it's the name of the drink," said the fairy.

"Coming right up." The bartender winked, and then she spun away, reaching for one of the bottles on the shelf behind her.

I scanned the display, enjoying the violet lights that made everything glow, including the contents of several unmarked bottles whose contents glowed more red than purple.

I decided I didn't want to know everything offered here.

"I'm Gwendolyn," said the fairy.

"Gem," I said. "Nice to meet you."

"Are you meeting anyone special tonight or just browsing?"

The openness of her question left me speechless, but she just patted my hand. Tiny chains lined with shim- mering jewels wrapped around her fingers and extended up her arms until they met her ivory sleeves. Everything about her shimmered and shone.

"It's all right. I remember my first Monster Ball. Even with the stories I'd heard, it was quite a shock seeing it all live and in color. Just remember that everything is your choice. You don't have to do anything you don't want to do."

That was debatable.

"And," she went on, "the best part is when it's over, you go right back to your life. No harm done. No strings attached."

"What happens at the ball stays at the ball," I said, repeating the line Rigo had used.

"Exactly." Gwendolyn nodded.

A drink appeared in front of me, and I sniffed it suspiciously.

"It's just absinthe with a little cherry grenadine."

"*Just* absinthe?" I repeated, slightly horrified.

I'd always heard fairies could really hold their liquor. I, on the other hand...

Gwendolyn grinned, obviously having fun with me. "Newbies are a riot," she called to the succubus behind the bar.

They both watched as I took my first sip.

"Not bad," I admitted as the flavors hit my tongue. The Pop Rocks rim was fun too—but I wasn't going to tell them that and sound like a total newb.

The succubus wandered off to take another order, and Gwendolyn pointed out the rest of the room while I sipped my drink. The candy popped and fizzed inside my mouth, making it hard to talk. Luckily, Gwendolyn was perfectly happy filling the silence.

KISS OF DEATH 213

"The other bar is there. Each bartender has a signature drink. You should try the Drunk Dancing Bears if you get a chance. It's yummy."

My brows rose. I wouldn't have pegged Gwendolyn for such a drinker with her innocent looks, but one could never tell. Especially at a party like this one. Besides, you couldn't be that innocent and still be this at ease at a party like The Monster Ball.

"What about those?" I asked, pointing to the darkened corners on the far side of the ballroom.

"Oh, yes. Privacy in public, as they say," Gwendolyn said. "The hanging silks are spelled to be soundproof." She wiggled her eyebrows. "See no evil. Hear no evil. Know what I mean?"

"Yep, I think I do," I said and took another swig of my drink.

Gwendolyn laughed and patted my arm. "It's harmless fun, darling. Listen, I'll see you around. Have fun tonight." She winked. "But not too much."

"Trust me, my definition of fun is boring compared to this," I called to her as she glided away, ivory slippers peeking out from underneath her matching dress.

Alone again, I scanned the ballroom and slowly sipped my drink. The room wasn't even full yet, but even with the crowd already gathered, my senses buzzed and my nerves stood on end. I'd never been in the presence of so many different supernaturals at once. The fact that no one was trying to eat anyone else—unwillingly, anyway—was a testament to the supernatural world's universal love of partying.

Did the SSF know all these creatures existed? Would I have to tell them?

From onstage, the music shifted and there was a brief lull with only the soft strains of the electric guitar pouring through the speakers.

"Hawkins, report," came Rigo's faint voice in my earpiece.

I nearly spilled my drink but recovered quickly. I'd almost forgotten the damned comm unit was in there considering how useless it had been over the noise.

I took a sip of my drink and used my glass to cover my lips as they moved. "No eyes on target yet," I said just as a new song began, drowning out the sound of my own voice.

Rigo's response was short and full of warning. "Keep looking. And don't..." The rest of it was lost to the noise as the drums were added.

I sighed. Even lodged inside my ear, the gadget did me no good over the volume of the party.

"Base, if you can hear me, FYI, I don't copy. I repeat, I don't copy. Too much noise." I waited to confirm a response.

The earpiece crackled but no intelligible sound came through.

"I'm going to look for the mark," I added.

My words were met with more static.

I huffed in frustration then refocused on what I'd come here to do. No one on the other end of my comms could help me, anyway. This was my mission.

I could do this.

It was time to find my mark and finish what I'd come to do.

Tossing a few bills on the bar next to my half-empty glass, I waved goodbye to the bartender and made my way farther into the ballroom. While I walked, I scanned the room again—this time for the single purpose of identifying any possible threats.

So far, I hadn't seen a single security guard, which meant the two gargoyles at the door were it. I'd noticed when I came in, they were very obviously unarmed, but then if the legends were true, they didn't need weapons.

They *were* the weapons.

That could either be good for me—backup if things turned south—or bad.

My eyes caught again on the darker corners of the ball-room where gauzy curtains obscured what lay inside. I squinted, using my fae sight to penetrate the curtains, but even with that I could only barely make out the shape of the beds set up inside. Silhouettes moved, but I couldn't make them out. Some sort of cloaking spell then.

I tested the air around the curtains for evidence of magic, but my fae senses couldn't pinpoint anything.

Which meant Rigo was probably right about the magic preventing violence too. Whoever had spelled this place was powerful if I couldn't pick up on them.

"See something you'd like to try?"

The voice jolted me more than I wanted to admit. And not just because I'd been too wrapped up in strategizing to notice someone had gotten close enough that his breath felt warm against my ear. Mostly that. But I also couldn't help the shiver at the sexy tone he used.

I covered up my surprise with a demure smile and turned to my new companion. "I'm only window shopping," I said lightly.

A pair of gleaming eyes stared back at me. They were ice-blue and bottomless, set into a hot-as-hell face and a rock-hard body. Even through the button-down shirt he wore, I could tell he was an impressive package underneath.

At my comment, his lips twitched then curved upward. "No harm in sampling the merchandise, is there?"

Our eyes met and held, and the unmistakable scent of lust rolled off him, nearly knocking my fae senses sideways. This guy wasn't just an animal shifter; he was a predator. An alpha of his kind. And I'd just made eye contact for way too long to be considered platonic to a beast like him.

Shit.

I shifted away a bit so that when I looked at him next, it didn't expose my throat or allow for any marking on his part. His gaze sharpened, and I knew he'd noticed. Oh well, better to be alive than polite.

"Sorry, I'm vegan," I said pointedly. "No animals for me."

His smirk took my breath away. "Well, if you get a craving for fresh meat," he said, his gaze raking over me in a not-subtle-at-all kind of way, "Come find me."

He strode off before I could argue. Or agree. Or jump his bones. I mean, if the menu looked like him, I wasn't against mixing business with pleasure.

Wow.

Milo would be doing a victory dance right now. Three months in the Tiff and none of those guys had tempted me. Then again, the male that had just walked away from me was in an entirely different league.

I was still watching his amazing ass when the music shifted again, this time into something slower. A few people exited the dance floor. Most of them went around me, but one figure stopped in front of me.

I looked up and into the face of my target: Kristoff Rasmussen, tech mogul, billionaire, and international slime ball. The image Rigo had shown me earlier had prepared me for the confident smirk set in a too-narrow face. What I hadn't counted on were the eyes. Black as midnight, soulless, and cruelly self-serving; I had no doubt Kristoff wasn't accustomed to the word "no" or "not interested." What he wanted, he took.

And tonight, he wanted me.

"Good evening, Mr. Rasmussen," I said in my best airhead voice.

The transition into my created persona was a skill I'd learned early during my training and one that came natural as a fae.

"Please, call me Kristoff." He took the hand I'd offered and rather than shake it, he pressed it to his lips and held it there. When he finally let me go, he stepped closer than was necessary and began his perusal.

I'd had men check me out before. Hell, Rigo did it daily, but this was beyond forward. He was already standing inside my personal bubble of space and with no attempt to hide it; he inspected me as if I were a menu. His gaze lingered so long on my chest, I had to resist the urge to remind him where my face was.

When he finally found my gaze again, his eyes gleamed with hunger—and fire. It was the tiniest of flames flickering back at me from inside slitted pupils. Barely a second and then it was gone. By the time he blinked again, his eyes looked normal, if not a little too wandering.

The flames I'd spotted wrapped inside a very animalistic stare were unmistakable, but just to be sure, I sniffed when he leaned close—and had to force my nose not to wrinkle.

Dammit. This guy was a fucking hellhound. What was

a demon offspring doing alive? Especially one the SSF knew about?

"You must be Lolita," he said, offering the assumed name Rodrigo's people had forged for me.

"Please, call me Lita," I said, pretending to enjoy the way his whiskey breath crowded my own supply of oxygen. *Ugh.* Why did men—particularly rich men—always assume they were exempt from basic manners and hygiene?

"Lita, then," he said. "You look absolutely stunning. Better than your picture." He inhaled and leaned in, grinning lasciviously as he added, "Your scent is already making me wonder what sort of details the photos your service provided—and that dress—are hiding."

I blinked. My scent?

Shit.

Hellhounds were known for their ability to sniff out... well, everything. Including things like dishonesty and manipulation. It was probably one of the things that had helped him climb so high on the corporate ladder or avoid getting taken out by SSF trackers. And fuck it all, it was really going to make this mission nearly impossible.

I bit back the rage that built for Rigo. He'd kept this from me on purpose, and it was going to cost him if it was the last thing I did. Instead, I plastered a flirty smile on my face and tried to conjure up some feeling of attraction or interest to cover up any scent that might suggest what I actually wanted from him. Yes, it was probably in his pants. No, it wasn't his doggy-dangler.

"A girl never tells," I said, complete with batting lashes.

Kristoff's smile turned smug. "Lucky for us, the night is young. There's plenty of time to uncover all of that." He winked, tucking my hand into his elbow as he began leading me toward the second bar. "Come. Let's get you a cocktail, and then you can tell me all about yourself."

Swallowing my disgust, I let myself be led away.

Kristoff stopped at the end of the bar and shoved aside another customer, ignoring the growl that rose up at our backs. I couldn't help but be a little impressed at the size of his balls when Kristoff didn't even bother to turn and face the werewolf he'd obviously pissed off. You had to be pretty sure of yourself to turn your back on an angry dog.

Or stupid.

The fae bartender closest to where we stood eyed Kristoff with raised brows. Clearly, he wasn't a fan of Kristoff's methods either. The male fae glanced at me, and his expression sharpened a bit.

Shit. That was all I needed. One of my own kind seeing straight through my glamour to the pointed ears hiding underneath.

"What can I get for you?" he asked.

"She'll have a Frostbite," Kristoff told him without bothering to ask me.

Poking out from underneath his silver hair, pointed

ears twitched as he strained to hear Kristoff's response. The bartender looked over at me, his silvery eyes clearly waiting for confirmation.

I sighed but nodded.

He pursed his lips and looked back at Kristoff. "And for you?" he asked him.

"Lemonade and fireball," Kristoff snapped.

The bartender didn't look too happy about his request, and I couldn't blame him. A hellhound with a fireball buzz didn't sound like a very friendly combination, but he went to work on the drinks without complaint.

While we waited, Kristoff's phone buzzed.

I pretended not to notice as he read a text. A second later, I watched from the corner of my eye as Kristoff nodded almost imperceptibly, his gaze fixed on something —or someone—behind me.

Before I could catch a glimpse, the bartender handed me a glass. I took it with a wobbly hand, letting some of the liquid slosh over the edge onto my wrist. The wince I gave at the chilled liquid wasn't forced. Holy shit, this drink was otherworldly cold. Too late, I realized the Frostbite portion undoubtedly came from the fae himself.

"Oh, dear, I'm so clumsy. Do you have a napkin?" I spun around, pretending to look for something to wipe my hand.

Sliding my gaze up, I caught sight of a man standing with his back to the wall not far from a dimly lit archway leading out of the ballroom. His dark hair was cropped close in a no-nonsense military buzz cut. He wore a suit similar to Kristoff's, but the sleeves strained around the man's thick muscles and the pants were two inches too short. Borrowed, clearly. Or just a bad sizing. Either way, considering the angry set to his jaw, I had a feeling the suit wasn't his usual attire.

He was obviously Kristoff's hired goon.

He caught me looking and glared back at me. I spun quickly to the bartender who held a napkin out. Smiling, I took it and wiped up the mess I'd made. Beside me, Kristoff was too wrapped up in his drink—and checking out everything with boobs—to notice my recon.

When I looked again, the man was still there, watching me.

So, Kristoff had brought a date.

Once I had a firm grip on my drink, Kristoff grabbed my hand again and began leading me back through the crowd. I didn't realize his destination until it was too late. By then, we'd already reached the u-shaped couches that lined the far wall. Kristoff let go of my hand long enough to sweep his arm out in a gesture for me to sit.

I chose a spot between two other couples, both locked in quiet conversations with one another. Still, I was glad we weren't alone at least. And even more relieved he hadn't chosen one of the curtained beds nearby. There was a lot I was willing to do for this mission, but sex with a client wasn't one of them.

Nerves twirling in my stomach, I set my purse aside and perched on the edge of the couch before taking a hefty swig of my drink.

This was it.

Time to get to work.

"So," Kristoff began, sitting close enough beside me that our legs were pressed together. I pretended not to mind it and resisted the urge to wrinkle my nose against the stench of his breath when he spoke again. The fireball was a lot stronger than the lemonade. "Tell me about yourself. What do you like to do for fun?"

"Well," I began, channeling Lita. "I like yummy drinks like this." I rattled the ice in my glass and grinned. "And I like parties and..." I cast a quick glance around the ballroom for something else to name.

There were plenty of amazing sights to choose from.

The creatures I saw milling around us or swaying to the music were stunning. Many of them had dropped any attempt at appearing human. Dresses had cutouts for tails that twitched in time to the bass while others had forgone clothes altogether in favor of small scraps of fabric to cover the important bits in order to let things like scales or fur hang out.

A few of them appeared human-like, though I knew

none of them really were. And none of them were paying a single shred of attention to me.

None except for one.

A tall, broad-shouldered figure stood at the edge of the dance floor, alone and unmoving among the others rocking and gliding. He wore a black suit complete with gloves and a black mask that looked out of place where everyone else had dropped their own disguises. The only bit of color was a blood-red bowtie.

For a moment, I wondered if he was the shifter who'd flirted with me earlier, but the eyes were completely different; dark, almost black, and bottomless. And the way he stood wasn't an alpha stance. If anything, it was beaten. Despite his set shoulders and the quiet confidence, he seemed defeated somehow. Or sad.

He gave no indication as to what kind of creature he was or what had made him stop moving. My fae senses were completely at a loss.

The only thing I knew for certain was that he was staring right at me.

I could feel it as surely as I felt Kristoff's weight lilting toward me on the tiny couch. Except the stranger's attention didn't make my skin crawl. In fact, his presence drew me in until I forgot all about the tech billionaire scuzbucket beside me.

"Yes?" Kristoff prompted, leaning in. I felt his gaze sweep down to my cleavage and then back up to my face as

I finally wrenched my eyes from the mysterious stranger. "What else do you like?"

"Um." I set my drink aside, trying to remember what I'd been about to say. The music pouring through the enormous speakers was making it hard to think. Or maybe it was my brain catching frostbite. Hells Angels, this drink was cold.

"Dancing," I said and shot to my feet just before Kristoff's mouth could brush my earlobe. "I love this song!"

I took a few steps toward the dance floor, scanning for the man I'd seen a moment ago. But he was gone.

A hand landed on my lower back, and the smell of fireball hit me as Kristoff whispered, "I only know how to slow dance. I hope that's all right."

Ugh. I rolled my eyes and led the way to the dance floor. It was perfect for what I needed to do, but I had a feeling I wasn't going to like the price.

The band was good, I noticed, casting a quick glance toward the stage. According to Starla, Dastardly Deeds had a reputation for putting entire parties on their ass thanks to Marina, the lead singer. Apparently, her siren song could make your feet move until well past their physical limits, leaving you sore at best. Dead at worst. I could only assume she'd taken her power down a notch for tonight since no one looked enthralled or on the verge of collapsing.

Still, there was a definite pull to sway to her song, and

it only got stronger the closer I got to where she stood onstage covered only by her long blue hair and a few crystal sequins. By the time I reached the dance floor, an open area with speakers pointed directly at the dancers, my entire body pulsed with the rhythm of the music.

I found an empty space on the floor and turned to find Kristoff close behind me. He reached for me eagerly and wrapped his hands around my waist, pulling me close. I wound an arm around his neck and let the other rest casually on his shoulder. His skin already felt hot to the touch, which for hellhounds was probably par for the course, but still.

Maybe if I didn't encourage him, he'd keep his hands—

Not even five seconds into our swaying, one of his hands dropped low, grazing my ass.

I gritted my teeth.

Kristoff's eyes met mine. He smiled suggestively. I smirked back at him.

All around us, couples moved and swayed, but Kristoff barely shuffled side to side. If his moves in bed were anything like his dancing, it was no wonder he had to pay for dates. Not that I ever planned to find out for sure.

I waited until at least a minute or two into our dance before I let my hands begin to wander. True to my assumption, the moment mine did, Kristoff's did too. I did my best to ignore the gentle rubbing over my hips and let my own hand drop to his waist, slinking around to hold him tighter as my fingers continued to idly brush over his jacket. In return, Kristoff's hand dropped lower too, brushing over the top of my ass for the second time.

I bit my tongue and kept up the charade.

Swaying a bit more heavily, I dropped my hand again, this time dipping my fingers into his front coat pocket.

Nothing.

Damn.

I slid my hand free again and worked it slowly up his chest before letting it rest on his shoulder. Then I repeated the whole thing with my left hand. Finally, my fingers closed over a small rectangular item.

I slid my fingers over it to be sure and was rewarded with three solid edges and a fourth hollow end—perfect for plugging into a tech device.

Thank the angel.

I closed my fist around the chip and slid it free, using my body to distract Kristoff. And while I hated everything about what I was doing, I couldn't help the tiny sense of victory. I'd gotten the chip without losing my dignity—well, not completely. I'd passed my test.

Next stop, detective.

But Kristoff wasn't done with me yet.

His swaying increased a bit and so did the pressure. Apparently all of my hand movements had been taken as an invitation for more intimate touching. He pressed into me, mostly with his already-hardened groin.

Ugh. Gross.

His hands on my hips tightened and one of them slid down to cup my ass.

I drew back, not even needing to fake the shock and outrage in my expression. "What do you think you're doing?" I demanded.

His thick brows drew together in confusion.

Before he could answer, I shoved him away, playing up the dramatics so that others would hear us. Hopefully, the embarrassment I'd cause him would make him think twice about trying to call me ever again—which would be a good thing since the phone number he had wouldn't work after tonight.

"We're just dancing," he sputtered.

"Last time I checked, dancing is more of a move-your-feet activity. Not your hands. Next time a girl agrees to a dance, keep your hands to yourself," I said loudly.

Then I spun on my heel, making sure to whip my hair in his face, and stalked off. The moment I was clear, I reached up and dropped the tech-chip into my bra for safe-keeping. Without missing a beat, I headed for the nearest exit. Party of the year or not, it was time to get the hell out of here.

The rest of my life was waiting.

NINETEEN

I ducked through the nearest archway, fingers crossed that the passageway led to an exit. Considering the magic that had brought me into the party, I wasn't sure if leaving was as simple as walking out the front door, but anywhere was better than the same room as the hellhound I'd just stolen from. Maybe if I got far enough from the noise, my earpiece would work to contact Rigo for a way out.

The walls of the stone hall were bare aside from the sconces mounted at regular intervals. Even those only put out just enough light to navigate around the next bend. This part of the castle was obviously not meant for loitering. The message was clear: the party was in the main ballroom and everyone should stick to that space.

Except that was now the one place I couldn't go.

But even here, the music still pulsed, and the smooth walls vibrated with the heavy drum beats. Underneath that, a current of energy—lust, if my fae senses were correct—wove its way through everything, growing stronger as I passed a narrow corridor wrapped in darkness.

"Base, come in," I said quietly as I walked.

No answer.

Either I was too deeply entrenched in magic here or Rigo had already given up on me.

I squinted into the blackness that seemed to swallow the passage, but the light didn't seem to penetrate beyond the opening. Strange. At least here, sconces and torches lit the way, but none of that light penetrated the smaller passageway.

I paused, letting my senses investigate what lay on the other side of the heavy door at the far end. Two bodies pressed tightly enough together they might as well be one. And none of the noises coming from inside sounded like a call for help.

Not an exit then.

Apparently, the curtained beds inside the ballroom *weren't* the only place for private partying.

Doubling back to the main corridor, I passed two women walking in the opposite direction. One of them studied me, obviously trying to catch my eye. I kept my head down and pretended not to notice her. I could only handle so many problems at once, and I damn sure couldn't afford for her to stop and chat with me. Her friend seemed less inclined to conversation, though, and they passed on without a word.

After another few steps, my ears twitched with some tiny sound.

My senses went on alert, and I paused to listen.

Behind me, footsteps approached. Heavy, steady—purposeful from the sound of it. Not some wanderer. And whoever it was, they were headed this way.

Shit.

If Kristoff's hound *had* scented more than an airhead with a sudden sense of self-worth, I was screwed—and not in the way he'd hoped for.

"You forgot to leave your shoe."

I sucked in a sharp breath as a familiar face rounded the bend. Not Kristoff. The other guy I'd rejected tonight. The one who'd flirted with me when I'd first arrived. Despite the danger I was running from, butterflies danced in my belly at the sight of his bright blue eyes fixed so intently on mine.

"My shoe?" I repeated, breathless at his closeness. He'd been handsome before, but now that I took the time to study him, he was traffic-stopping hot.

He pointed to my feet. "If you're going to pull a Cinderella and run out of the ball so early, you're supposed to leave your shoe behind. It'll make it easier to hunt you down later."

"And what if I don't want to be hunted down?"

He stepped closer, an easy smile on his tanned face. "Every girl wants to be hunted."

I shook my head. "Does that line actually work for you?"

He shrugged. "You tell me."

When he leaned in again, I held up a hand to stop him. "Uh-uh. You're cute, but it's not that easy. And neither am I."

A smile played on his delicious mouth. "Yes, I think you made that point crystal clear for the entire dance floor. No one out there thinks you're easy."

I bit my lip, cringing at the idea that so many might have seen my show with Kristoff. "The entire dance floor?" I repeated.

"Relax. It took you off their radar, which I suspect is what you wanted in the first place." He cocked his head, studying me. "Tell me, why does a girl who doesn't want company come to a party like this one, anyway?"

"I told you. Window shopping."

He laughed, a deep, rich sound that sent a shiver down my spine. "Funny, you don't strike me as the type to look when you don't plan to touch."

Heat crept up my throat and into my cheeks as I imagined touching him the way I'd touched Kristoff. Roaming hands, swaying bodies, torsos pressed tight—

"You also had me pegged for the Cinderella type," I shot back before the fantasy blurred right into reality. "Just goes to show you don't know nearly as much about me as you think you do."

He leaned in close until I was backed against the wall. My shoulders hit the cold, smooth stone, and I was glad for the way it cooled the heat already building underneath my skin. It wasn't fair how hot he could make me with just those eyes.

Slowly, he reached up and placed a hand on either side of my head, trapping me. I had no doubt he'd back off if I told him to, but the words died on my tongue before I could say them. My mouth went dry, and I couldn't seem to tear myself from his gaze.

"You're right. I don't know you at all," he said quietly. A predator sizing up its prey. "But I'd like to."

His lips brushed my jawline in a kiss that was clearly meant as an invitation. I shuddered, my skin tingling deliciously where his lips had grazed.

How long had it been since I'd let someone touch me like this? Six months? Seven? Hell, if I didn't get ahold of my own willpower, I was going to combust long before we even arrived at the main event.

"Shouldn't we start with introductions?" I murmured, leaning into his mouth where it was nuzzling at my ear. God, this guy was an animal. I wondered how that translated to his sexual prowess and another shudder shook my shoulders. I reached up and grabbed his shirt, a little embarrassed at myself for it.

"I'm Jax McGuire. And you are?"

Turned on. "Gem Hawkins."

The words were out before I could stop them. Shit. Not my real name. What in the hell was I thinking?

Right. I wasn't thinking. Not with my brain anyway.

Jax pressed another kiss to my jawline, this one farther back, near my ear. "It's nice to meet you, Gem Hawkins," he whispered.

His hands landed on my hips and then quickly swept upward. Fingertips grazed my breasts, and I let my head fall backward. "Oh, it's nice... to meet..." I tried responding and then gave up, completely lost in the sensations of his hands on me. "So nice," I panted.

He laughed and the deep, rich sound of it sent warmth straight through my core.

"Not fair," I said as his mouth left a trail of kisses down my exposed throat. His hands touched and teased as they worked my breasts. Through the thin fabric of the dress, his thumb found my already-pointed nipples. When he flicked lightly, I moaned again.

"This?" he asked innocently. "This isn't fair?"

"No, this is very... Okay, I'll allow it," I said, and he laughed again.

"That," I insisted, reaching out to run my own hands over his broad chest. Even through the fabric of his shirt, I could feel the hard lines of defined muscle. "That laugh," I insisted. "It's entirely too sexy. Cheating."

He raised his head so that we were eye to eye now. His lids were heavy, his blue eyes intense with desire. One of his hands wound around the small of my back, pulling me toward him until we were pressed tightly together in all the right places.

"Shut me up then," he growled.

I lifted onto my toes, arching toward him.

The moment I started to move, he closed the distance, and if not for his arm holding me up, I would have liquefied and melted into a puddle right there. His mouth was hot and urgent on mine. There was no hesitation, no soft request for permission. Only heat and need and a demand that I offer whatever he wanted from me.

Any other man would have been swiftly ass-kicked for such a move. Z sure had. But right now, all I wanted was to surrender and let this sexy stranger take every single gift I had to offer.

So much for no distractions.

Lust curled inside me, aching and straining as I clung to him. One hand fisted in his shirt. The other wound around his neck, pulling him even closer as our mouths pushed and pulled at the other. His hand grazed my breast before dropping low to trace my thigh. His fingers trailed a line upward, dipping underneath the hem of my dress. I panted into his mouth, rocking my hips into his hand, nearly desperate with need.

He pulled his hand back and eased his mouth from

mine just enough to say, "Why don't we take this party somewhere more private so we can get to know each other?"

I blinked to clear the fog and make sense of his words.

Angel balls.

He meant one of those dark rooms I'd passed; the ones with all the noises coming from inside. "I..."

Jax straightened, leaning away from me. His hand dropped into mine, tugging me along. "Come on. I know a place."

In the space he'd left between us, a gust of fresh air—and clarity—hit me. What the hell was I about to agree to? A quickie in a broom closet was one thing, but I was on an active mission.

I looked up at Jax, still trying to lead me away.

He was so damn sure of himself. A man who was used to getting what—and who—he wanted. And apparently, he'd decided he wanted me. My body ached to let him have me. But we weren't even past first base and already I was losing control.

Something I couldn't afford to do. Not tonight anyway.

"Jax." I pulled away, almost positive I was going to regret this later.

He turned back, his intense blue eyes nearly eating right through my resolve. "What's up, gorgeous?"

Definitely going to regret this later. "I think I need to take a rain check."

He didn't falter an inch. If anything, his grin only grew wider, more knowing. He stepped close again and kissed my cheek, this time without all the pheromones he'd unleashed on me earlier.

"Darling," he said, "I expected nothing less." Then he let go of my hand and backed away.

My eyes narrowed. "Really? That's it? You're giving up?"

He winked as he retreated backward. "Not even close. We'll meet again, Gem Hawkins, and I won't need a shoe to find you."

I watched as he turned and disappeared back the way he'd come, his hips literally swaying with swagger. For the second time tonight, I was speechless at the sight of his perfect ass.

How had I just said no to that?

I hated myself already.

No, I hated Rigo. He definitely deserved another punch for what I'd just thrown away. It was time to find him and deliver.

TWENTY

Alone once again, I made it far enough down the hallway that the noise of the music faded behind me. Hopefully that meant I was nearing an exit, although my senses told me I'd somehow managed to wander farther than the magic wanted. A musty smell hung in the air, and the lights seemed dimmer this way. It was looking more and more like I wasn't getting out of here without Rigo's help. Maybe that's how he'd wanted it all along.

"Hawkins to base, do you copy?"

I wiggled my earpiece, hoping the interference from the speakers inside hadn't totally fried the connection. The recruits always got hand-me-down gear, and the comms were straight up shit on the best days.

"Recruit to base, do you copy?" I repeated when no answer came.

I sighed and then reminded myself tonight was the last

night I'd ever have to deal with shoddy equipment. Or Rigo for that matter. The SSF detective division provided their agents with only the best, most advanced gear, including comms and anything else required by the mission.

My access to the answers I wanted had never felt so close.

I took a right at the next intersection—a route that would take me farther away from the party—and kept walking, sticking to the outside of the hallway as it curved around. Was this entire passageway one big circle then? It was a fun design but not very practical when one didn't want to be seen.

There were no corners.

"Base to Hawkins, I read you." Rigo's voice spilled into my ear unexpectedly enough to make my heart leap. It was the one and only time I was glad to hear Rigo's nasally tone. "Do you have the package?"

"I'm safe, thanks for asking," I said with an eye roll.

"Of course you are," Rigo replied. "We wouldn't have sent you in if we weren't confident—"

"My ass, Rigo," I cut him off. "Why didn't you tell me that asshole was a hellhound?" I hissed. "Is this your way of getting back at me?"

When Rigo spoke again, his voice was tight. "Do you have the package or not?"

"Yes, I have the—"

The fist came out of nowhere and caught me square in the jaw.

Lights exploded behind my eyes as pain lit up every inch of my face. I was thrown backward and spun until my shoulder slammed against the wall. I hit the cold concrete hard, grunting as my breath whooshed out. Pain radiated from my cheek all the way to the top of my scalp.

I blinked and cast a quick glance at my attacker.

Surprise—and then a fair amount of dread—washed over me as I recognized the man who'd hit me. It was the brick wall of a security guard I'd spotted earlier. Kristoff's "plus one."

And his right hook was about to be followed up by his left.

I ducked just in time to avoid a second blow but moving far enough out of his reach was a bit trickier thanks to my precarious heels. The man came at me again. Instead of dodging away, I smashed my fist into his nose. There was a small crack as I felt his flesh and bone give underneath my knuckles. The monster of a man stumbled back a step, shook his head as if to clear it, then came for me again.

Shit.

He was like one of those cartoons who saw birdies floating around their heads after they got hit. Those assholes always got right back up again. It wasn't fair.

I managed to block the next swing—thankfully his massive size meant he was a little slower than me—but the one after that landed. My shoulder seized up at the force of his fist, and I let out a small sound of pain.

By the angel, this guy was a brickhouse.

Before I could recover, his hand closed over my throat and squeezed. I struggled against him, gagging, but he had me pinned against the wall and no amount of scraping or hitting loosed him.

That magic Rigo had mentioned to me earlier—the spell work preventing violence—would be a nice surprise right about now...

Or was it only death it prevented?

I couldn't remember, but the idea of spending the next few hours as this guy's punching bag made death sound sort of appealing.

Finally, I kicked out in desperation, and my pointed toe landed hard against his groin. He groaned and released me so that he could stumble away, holding his hands delicately over the injured area.

The sudden imbalance sent me reeling. I managed to catch myself and turned away, ready to sprint for the doors —wherever they were—but another figure stood in my way, blocking my exit.

"Lita, where are you going in such a hurry? Don't you know it's rude to run out on a date this way?" Kristoff's eyes narrowed shrewdly as he studied me, the dim sconces on the wall reflecting off the light in his pupils. Like earlier, a tiny flame flickered in his irises.

I didn't answer, mostly because I was too caught up in trying to breathe again, and my throat hurt like it had just been set on fire and left to burn.

In my earpiece, Rigo's voice was frantic. I'd ignored it for most of the fight, but now he was nearly screaming, "Base to Hawkins. What the hell is going on? Report!"

Kristoff strode forward, his creepy gaze locked on my chest as it rose and fell heavily. When he got close enough, he reached for my face. I forced myself not to flinch as I prepared for some kind of attack. Instead, he grabbed my comm unit and snatched it out of my ear.

"I can see why you're so distracted," he said, my comm caught between his thumb and forefinger. "You came here to meet me, but you've already let another man get inside your head." He dropped the earpiece to the floor and crushed it with the heel of his shoe.

I pursed my lips, my expression carefully unaffected by the fact that he'd just exposed me. "I don't think things are going to work out between us, Kristoff. You don't trust me at all."

He let out a snarl and leaned in close. "You will return what you took from me, or I will take it from you by force."

His stale breath washed over me, nearly gagging me all over again. Out of the corner of my eye, I saw Kristoff's muscle edging closer. Kristoff and the man shared a glance, and I knew muscles-for-brains was just waiting on the signal before he grabbed me and started in on round two.

I kept my expression carefully neutral, but inside, my heart thudded heavily against my chest. Fucking A. I was burned, and there wasn't a damn thing base could or would do about it. They'd made that fact crystal clear. Either I found a way out on my own or Kristoff would drag me home to do whatever he wanted when the protective magic was gone.

"Tell you what," I said, meeting Kristoff's gaze with the steeliest stare I could muster. "You tell shit-for-brains over there to take a walk," I nodded my head at Kristoff's guard dog then softened my voice, "and I'm sure you and I can come to an understanding."

Kristoff huffed, not even a scrap of hesitation in him before he smirked and said, "Haven't you heard? This is a party. And three's a crowd."

He shoved his knee into my stomach, and I doubled over, groaning.

Thick hands grabbed me from behind, yanking me into the unlit passageway at my back. Within seconds, the darkness had swallowed us up. I screamed, knowing it was the only chance I had left. The sound of my voice echoed, bouncing off the concrete walls surrounding me as if even it couldn't reach beyond the dark passageway.

"Scream all you like," Kristoff said. "Plenty of other guests here tonight are doing the same for their own reasons. Yours won't have much effect."

A hand gripped my hair, yanking hard, and I stumbled

backward, dragged farther into the blackness of the passageway. Desperation clawed at me. I twisted and swung out, my fist connecting with a meaty arm, but it wasn't enough to break the hold. I swung out a second time. This time, when my knuckles met his skin, pain ricocheted up my arm as my hand met with a hard surface. It felt more like stone than skin. What the hell was this freak?

Gargoyle, maybe?

Whatever he was, my fists weren't making a dent.

A second later, we rounded a narrow doorway, and I yelped as the hand let me go with enough force to fling me against the wall of a small, dark room. Whatever light had reached us from the main hall was gone now.

Pitch darkness closed in around me, and I blinked, sucking in gulps of air that tasted way too stale for this room to be anything but forgotten.

My fae senses kicked in, my sight sharpening almost instantly.

Two shadows loomed in front of me, but neither one seemed put off by the darkness. I could only assume they both had the same night vision I did. Between that and Mr. Stone-for-Skin, I was going to have to up my game if I wanted to get out of this in one piece.

We were about to test just how strong all this spell work really was.

For a split second, I was tempted to go with a carbon copy of rocks-for-brains, give him a taste of his own medicine, but it would have taken too long. I needed strength now. And there was only one creature I could conjure without concentration.

My face changed first.

The familiar stretching and popping filled the air as my facial features warped. My nose elongated, bones cracking as a giant beak formed. Then my ears vanished underneath a thick layer of feathers and down. The feathers spread from the top of my head down to my chest, covering every inch of skin in its wake.

My arms turned to wings, stretching and widening— and threatening to topple me if I didn't hold them correctly.

"No," Kristoff growled, lunging for me. "She's changing. Stop her."

I swayed hard to the right. Thanks to my wing position and my half-shifted body, Kristoff's lackey was on me before I could evade him. A meaty hand wrapped around my throat. My beast squawked and squealed at the pressure, clawing harder to find a release.

Kristoff loomed in front of me, his fingers fumbling with a small vial he'd produced from who knew where. I'd checked his pockets earlier and hadn't felt anything like that inside them. Before I could speculate what he'd smuggled in here, he was uncapping it and emptying the contents into my half-open beak.

I writhed away from him, but there was nowhere to go,

not with the vise grip around my throat holding me in place. Too late, I remembered the silly "weapon" Rodrigo had stowed inside my purse—and the fact that I'd left my purse on that couch inside the ballroom.

Dammit.

So much for smuggling things in under the radar.

The mystery liquid, warm and thick, coated my eagle tongue. Within seconds, my inner beast stalled and then receded altogether. My human form reappeared, my bones aching at the half-shift they'd been forced back from.

"What the hell...?" I managed in a choked voice.

"What's the matter? Not feeling like yourself?" Kristoff asked and then laughed at his own joke.

"What did you give me?" I demanded.

"Just a little something to keep you out here and whatever's inside you in there," he said, an edge to his words.

I strained, searching through my mind for some sign of my inner creature, but it was just gone. Desperate, I tried shifting into my mother instead. Her fae body was the second easiest form I could take.

But that one didn't work either.

Staring hard at the man holding me in his clenched hand, I gathered my strength and used everything I had left on one last attempt. It had always been easier to mimic a subject when I had them in my sights.

I felt my skin ripple and my flesh stretch as my face

changed. The goon holding me blanched, and I knew my features had morphed enough for him to see my goal.

"Boss, she's...me."

"Yes, I can see that," came Kristoff's reply.

The grip around my throat loosened slightly. "But how?"

"She's a shapeshifter, you idiot. She can look like anything she wants," Kristoff said.

I couldn't, actually. Not anything. But there was no point in telling either of them that.

Glaring at my doppelgänger, I gritted my teeth and willed the change to completely take me over. If I had to look like this guy in order to beat them, so be it. Although, if Rigo asked, I was going to maintain I'd beaten them with my disguise intact and let that be the end of it.

But just as quickly as the change had come, it vanished again. This time, it left behind a strange burning in my stomach. And underneath that, an emptiness. I knew without even trying to draw on it, there was nothing left.

No magic.

No ability to shift.

Nothing.

"What the hell did you give me?" I demanded again.

"A cocktail," Kristoff replied vaguely.

Fear lanced through me, but I shoved it away. Panic would only cripple me now. I had to think straight for as long as that drink would let me.

"Poison?" I asked.

"Just something to level the playing field," Kristoff said smugly.

I glared at him. "Hardly level when you still have the power to change and I don't."

"I have no intention of changing. Not when this form is capable of having so much more fun with you." Even as he said it, his eyes rippled again with the flash of flames I'd seen earlier. "Women," he snorted to his friend. "Always wanting a man to change for her."

The goon frowned at me, but it wasn't much more than a murky line where his mouth had drawn down. With my fae sight gone, I could barely make out his face in the dark room. That scared me more than these two assholes. The Tiff's magic-stripping aside, not once in my whole life had my extra senses failed me. But they were failing me now. No matter how hard I tried, I couldn't call up a single remnant of my beast or my fae traits.

Thanks to that drink Kristoff had forced on me, my eyesight had dimmed, my strength had dwindled. All my power was gone. It was the liquid equivalent of the Tiff's magic-stripping wards.

Kristoff watched me, his lips twisted weirdly in cruel enjoyment. "How does it feel to be robbed of something so important to you?"

"Kiss my ass," I snarled at him, straining against the hand that held me by the throat.

"What a delicious invitation," Kristoff whispered. He turned to his minion and snapped, "Hold her still no matter what."

Kristoff's hands landed on my chest, fingers exploring the seam where fabric met skin. His fingers pawed at my breasts, and I had to swallow the bile that rose in my throat. With a disgusting smirk, Kristoff reached into my dress and drew out the tiny chip I'd stashed earlier.

"Bingo." He held it up then slid it into the pocket of his pants.

"Fuck you," I muttered.

Kristoff's palm shot out, landing with a hard crack across my cheek.

I gritted my teeth as pain radiated up to my temple.

"Boss," warned the brute. "We can't leave evidence. You know what happens to party guests who break the rules."

Kristoff grunted. "Calm down, Feldspar. We aren't going to kill her," he said as if that made all of this okay.

Feldspar? That was unfortunate even for an asshole like him.

"What if the proprietor comes?" Feldspar sounded less and less sure about their plan.

"The proprietor doesn't give a shit about us," Kristoff shot back, but there was a hint of uncertainty that hadn't been there before.

Huh. So there was at least one person Kristoff was afraid of.

"Hey, Kristoff," I said, my voice low and throaty, and not just because my neck was being squeezed. "I think you're on to something."

Kristoff leaned in—way too sure of himself to be cautious now. "What are you talking about, wench?"

"I just wanted to say that you were right," I said, wheezing through the words.

"Right about what?" Now his hand was rubbing the length of my arm.

"As long as you don't kill, you haven't broken the rules." I brought my knee up as hard as I could into his groin.

Kristoff screamed—a long, high-pitched keening sound that was more beast than man—and went down to one knee.

The hand squeezing my throat released me. I sucked in a couple of unhindered gulps of air and then rounded on my opponent. Kristoff was bent over at the waist, one hand braced on the floor for balance as he continued to howl. Feldspar stood beside him looking torn about whether to try to help his boss somehow or pummel me.

"Boss?" Feldspar asked uncertainly.

I couldn't help the satisfied smirk that ghosted my lips. "Did you get everything you wanted from me or shall I keep dishing it out?"

Kristoff shot me a look, still hunched over. Then he turned to Feldspar. "Kill the bitch. We'll worry about the rules later."

Feldspar straightened, his hands fisting the moment the order was given. He took a step toward me.

I backed up and hit the wall.

Feldspar closed in, and no matter how much I strained to call up my inner beast, no answer came. I was on my own here.

"Angel balls," I muttered just as Feldspar raised a stone-cold fist and swung.

TWENTY-ONE

In the split second it took me to duck away from Feldspar's outstretched fist, someone screamed. It sounded like Kristoff. Except that I hadn't touched him. Stepping out of my shoes, I slid silently along the wall to the far side of the room, hoping the inky darkness would provide enough cover to at least slow down my attacker. Maybe if I was quick, I could slip past him and out the door.

Straight ahead, in the open doorway, something moved. A shadow or a silhouette—Feldspar blotted it out before I could be sure.

I sucked in a gulp of air and kept weaving.

On the floor, Kristoff writhed. I tried to figure out what had sent him into another fit of pain, but my own problems were much more urgent.

I was forced backward again by Feldspar, both of us grunting with our efforts. He finally wised up to my defensive maneuvers, and instead of swinging sideways, he stepped forward, closing the distance between us until it was impossible for me to slip away again.

He reached for me. Instead of landing another blow, he grabbed a fistful of my hair, yanking until I was on my tiptoes before him.

From behind him came a small noise.

A piece of fabric? The shuffle of quiet feet?

Feldspar must have heard it too because he hesitated, turning his head only slightly at the tiny sound.

It was all I needed.

Bending at the knees, I dropped straight down and thrust my hands out, feeling around on the dark floor. My hand closed over one of the shoes I'd abandoned earlier. I grabbed it and yanked it—and myself—back up to where Feldspar waited above me.

His hands grabbed my arms.

I brought the shoe up and then back down again as hard as I could. The tip of the heel sank into Feldspar's eye.

He let out a howl, stumbling away and pulling desperately on the shoe. It made a disgusting sound of wet suction as he wrenched it free. With a snarl, he chucked the shoe across the room and spun toward me. Blood and fluid oozed from his injury.

I ducked out of his reach, intent on making it through

the door, but Feldspar was faster. He grabbed me by the shoulders, shoving me backward.

I hit the wall with a thud, sending a crack through my shoulder blades.

The air whooshed out of my lungs, and Feldspar closed the distance between us. My shoulders sagged. Whatever he had planned, I knew I wasn't going to be able to stop him. With my fae energy gone and no ability to shift, I was at his mercy.

Maybe it would have been better if he *had* been able to smuggle in a weapon. Or if the magic would just let him strangle me. Hours of this was going to feel like torture. Not to mention the level of grossness at having to stare at his leaking eye through the whole thing.

But then the air changed again—another rustling of fabric. This time, with a distinctive shuffling of feet. Feldspar was grabbed from behind and thrown across the room like a weightless doll. He crashed into the far wall before slumping heavily to the floor. Dust and stone rained down around him.

Feldspar groaned but didn't try to get up.

Kristoff climbed slowly to his feet, and I spotted the shadowy outline of another man behind him.

"This is a private party," Kristoff said through clenched teeth. "You weren't invited." Even without my heightened senses, I could smell the blood on him that hadn't been there before. The stranger had hurt him—for me.

"Seems like the lady isn't looking to party with you," said a voice I'd never heard before. His words were calm enough, but there was an edge to his voice that made me stay where I was. Even if he was here to help me for some reason, every inch of him seemed ready and able to kill, magic or not.

Kristoff snorted. "She's not a lady. She's an agent. No, not even that. A recruit." He spit the last word.

Shock rippled through me hard enough to make me forget to be insulted. How did he know all of that?

"Even so, she's not here willingly. And you're hurting her. You know the rules," the stranger said.

"Who the hell are you to tell me the rules?" Kristoff demanded. He took a step toward the stranger, hunching over as he moved.

My muscles tensed because I knew what that stance meant. Kristoff was on the verge of shifting into his hound.

In answer, I tried again to call up my own beast. Still nothing.

Dammit.

"Let's just say I'm her guardian angel." This time, there was a sardonic lilt to the words that made me even more curious about the identity of my rescuer.

"She owed me a debt," Kristoff said. "This is none of your business."

"The debt has been more than paid," the stranger said. "Now, I'll collect the overages—in blood."

Kristoff roared, his body curling into itself until he was forced onto all fours. By the time his palms landed on the floor, hair had sprouted up and down the length of his body. Fingers changed into paws while a snout replaced his nose.

Eyes, beady and black with irises full of hellfire, stared back at me.

Then they swung to the stranger, and the hellhound growled low.

The stranger looked up at me then over to where Feldspar was just climbing to his feet. An unspoken question passed between us, and I felt the first stirrings of my fae strength begin to return. Relief surged through me followed quickly by grim determination.

"One for you, one for me?" I suggested.

The stranger didn't respond before Kristoff leaped at him, sending both of them tumbling into the hall.

That settled that.

Feldspar moved toward me, and I met him with a fist of my own. Stone scraped against stone as my half-shifted knuckles collided with his jaw, driving him backward.

Feldspar straightened and stared at me in confusion. "What the...?"

"Looks like your boss's cocktail has worn off. In my hands at least. How does it feel to get punched by your own stony knuckles?"

Feldspar roared and charged.

We traded blows with me mostly dancing away from him until my shifting ability finally worked its way up to full strength again. When it finally did, I let it happen faster than my bones could keep up. The beast inside me roared and stone fists were replaced almost instantly by talons and claws. I dropped to all fours and drove my beak upward, using it to nip and stab at my opponent.

At the sight of a monstrous griffin before him, Feldspar faltered, hesitating when it mattered. I planted my weight forward, using my talons to brace myself as I swung out with my back paw. My lion's claw caught his torso just below his heart, and I ripped him open with a jagged slash. Blood pooled and poured from the wound and Feldspar toppled to his knees.

His shoulders sagged as he stared down at the hole I'd left in him.

For once, I was glad for the darkness. I didn't want to see all the things leaking out of him just now.

"You can't...kill me," he managed, blood leaking from his mouth as he spoke the words. "The magic prevents death at the ball."

I shifted back to my human form—complete with the red dress and blonde hair. "No, but I just made you wish you were dead."

As if to punctate my words, Feldspar's legs gave out, and he fell with a thud.

I stood over him, grim with the carnage I'd caused. "I wouldn't make any sudden movements if I were you."

"You won't get away," he began, but I was already out the door.

The light from the main hall slanted dimly, washing everything in a barely there glow. I glanced down and saw Kristoff's hellhound claws had left a trail of blood. At the far end of the hall, he stalked toward his prey who currently stood way too calmly near the mouth of the passage.

I hurried forward, but when I got close enough to make out the stranger's features, I stopped in surprise. Same black and white suit I'd seen earlier in the ballroom. Same blood-red bow tie. Same mask covering his face. I'd seen him only for a second in the main ballroom, but it was him. I was sure of it.

"You," I said.

The masked man's gaze jerked toward mine.

Kristoff did the same, his fiery eyes narrowing when he spotted me. He doubled back and abandoned any patience he'd had before.

This time, there was no slow stalking.

He ran straight toward me, his mouth open and teeth bared.

I threw my arms into the air as he leaped at me, concentrating hard on the change. Feathers sprouted instantly down the length of my arms. My talons jutted through the tips of my fingers just in time.

I managed to sink a talon into Kristoff's throat, catching him and tossing him aside. We went down in a heap, rolling and biting at each other. My beast roared and squawked as I fought to shove the hellhound off me, but my shift was only half-complete. It was all I could do to keep the hound's claws and teeth from ripping into my very human throat.

On top of me, Kristoff went stiff and let out a keening howl before jumping off me and whirling at something behind him. I sat up in time to see Kristoff running in circles, teeth nipping at the high heel protruding from his flank.

The masked man stood over me, offering a bloody hand.

My brows shot up.

He shrugged. "It worked for you."

Without a word, I put my hand in his and let him pull me to my feet.

At the far end of the hall, Kristoff spun wildly in an attempt to use his sharpened teeth to pull the shoe out of his flesh. We had about two minutes before he managed it, and then I had a feeling round two was going to be hell.

"Are you all right?" the masked man asked.

"Who are you?" I demanded.

He hesitated, and then said simply, "A friend."

Not a good enough answer, but we'd circle back to that. "How did you find me down here?"

"The squawking," he said simply.

My eyes narrowed at the laughter in his voice. Was he mocking me?

"Relax," he said before I could unleash the torrent of curses already on the tip of my tongue. "The squawking saved your life. Here, I believe this is yours."

He dropped something into my hand. It took me a moment to realize what it was. My broken comm unit.

I angled away and tucked it into the front of my dress before turning back to him. Anxiety had wound its way through me, curling into a tight ball in the pit of my stomach. Every single one of them knew who and what I was. How in the hell was I going to fix this?

"He's not going to stop, is he?" I asked.

"His beast has the scent of your blood. Once that happens..." He didn't finish, but I already knew there was no stopping a hellhound with a vendetta.

My stomach knotted at the idea of Kristoff Rasmussen out for vengeance. I couldn't afford to fail this mission, but I also couldn't afford for Kristoff to burn me, either. And considering how much he knew about me, I had no doubt he would come looking for me once the constraints of the ball's magic no longer held him.

"I can't kill them," I said quietly.

The masked stranger's ensuing silence spoke volumes.

"How do I get around the magic preventing death?" I asked. Something told me if anyone knew the answer, it was this guy.

"You can't. Not in the castle, anyway."

I looked up at him sharply, studying the way his eyes seemed to fade right into the darkness of the space. Like he wasn't even here at all. "And outside of the castle?"

His mouth tightened into a thin line, and I knew he was weighing whether or not to tell me.

"If I don't kill him, he'll kill me," I said. "Tomorrow. Or next month. He'll come for me, and you know it."

"The magic applies to the castle grounds only," he said finally.

"And off castle grounds?" I prompted impatiently.

He finally cut me a sideways look. "I have an idea," he said. "You'll have to trust me."

Any sarcastic response I might have offered was cut short by the hellhound's victory cry. Kristoff had finally torn the shoe free from his flesh and was now charging at us, fangs exposed and eyes full of flames.

I called my beast and planted my feet, prepared to fight.

Before I could get close, the masked man stepped in front of me. His hand shot out and smashed into Kristoff's face. Bones snapped, and Kristoff yelped as he fell to the ground in front of me. The man reached down and wrapped his hand around Kristoff's throat, squeezing hard enough that no sound came from the hound's open mouth.

"No harm shall come to this girl," the man said, his voice booming so loudly, I had to fight the urge to cover my ears. Every fae sense I had was tingling at the raw power rolling off him.

I waited for the hellhound to fight back—to at least try to break the man's grip on his throat. But he only shuddered and shrank back as if hoping the floor would swallow him up.

I stared at the man crouched in front of me, suspicious and a little leery. Whatever he was, my fae senses couldn't read him, and that meant he was something beyond my power. It should have made me pause or even change my mind about accepting his help, but I had no choice. Kristoff was deferring to this man for the moment, but nothing would stop him from hunting me later. Whoever this guy was, tonight he was going to help me kill Kristoff Rasmussen.

TWENTY-TWO

Fog licked at my feet, wrapping everything in a blanket and leaving my skin slick with dew. Or maybe it was perspiration. I hadn't counted on a workout tonight—but then I also hadn't counted on having to commit murder either. Rigo would have to understand. I wasn't going to let Kristoff go only to have him show up later and catch me off guard.

This had to end now.

Beside me, the masked mystery man didn't even sound winded. Despite the heavy load he carried in his arms, his steps remained light and silent. Then again, thanks to my new form, I wasn't exactly straining under the weight of my load either.

My shifting ability was once again in full effect.

Good thing since we had to zigzag our way along, keeping to the outer edges to avoid being spotted by the guests that loitered out here. Not that any of them were doing much people watching. Most were too busy pawing at each other to notice us even without the fog obscuring the view.

I wondered what my new friend thought of all the public displays. Or what he was doing here at all. He didn't seem like the type who enjoyed these things. He also hadn't asked me how it was possible that I could shift into more than one beast. I could only assume that meant he had plenty of secrets of his own.

"Almost there," mystery man said.

I grunted a response, my voice low and deep thanks to the shift I'd made in order to handle the trek we were making. My doppelgänger, Feldspar, who I'd slung over my shoulder like a sack of potatoes, made a similar grunting noise—only his sounded a lot less coherent.

The back of my legs itched thanks to the blood running down them. I did my best not to think about the mess I'd made of Feldspar's innards or the trail of blood we'd probably left from that dark hallway to the moonlit lawn.

"Where are we going, anyway?" I asked. "Isn't there more cover if we head for those trees?" I nodded toward the left, but the masked man just shook his head.

"The property line ends just ahead."

Underneath my feet, the grass turned to hard-packed clay and rock, and then the earth disappeared into thin air just past a sheer drop-off.

Mystery man glanced toward the castle at our backs and then hurried to the cliff's edge, Kristoff's unconscious form hanging limp in his arms. When he was in position, he looked over at me. If he was put off by the fact that I looked like an exact copy of Feldspar the Furious, he didn't let on.

"You sure you want to do this?" he asked.

"You're getting cold feet *now*?"

"Of course not. I just want to make sure you know what you're doing. There will be consequences for taking a life." His eyes clouded. "There always is."

That might have been true, but the consequences for letting Kristoff live were just as bad. "I know what I'm doing."

He nodded at Feldspar dangling over my back. "Then you go first."

I did a quick mental check. The data chip I'd come for was once again tucked safely inside the front of my dress. Right next to my broken comm unit. I didn't even want to think about how crazy Rigo was going to be when I finally got back to the Tiff. My purse was a lost cause, but that was fine. There wasn't anything identifying in it.

"Ready?" mystery man asked.

I adjusted my grip on Feldspar. He'd lost enough blood and eye guts at this point that he wasn't even trying to fight me. Maybe it was because of that, but I hesitated.

"You don't have to do this," mystery man said quietly.

I bit my lip. "I know."

Another moment of silence passed between us. We were running out of time. I knew it and still I couldn't make myself finish it.

They weren't fighting back anymore. Suddenly, it didn't feel like self-defense. It felt like murder.

"Set him on the ground."

I looked up sharply and found mystery man's eyes nearly black again, like they'd been earlier in the hall. Pure violence lived in that look, and I couldn't help but shrink back a little.

"What are you going to do?" I asked.

"What needs to be done."

I didn't ask what that meant.

Lowering Feldspar to the ground, I tipped him forward until he landed in the grass in a heap. Blood coated his entire upper body, blotting out his face. I looked away, my stomach rolling.

The man dropped Kristoff unceremoniously next to Feldspar. Then he turned to me. "I want you to turn around and walk back inside. When you get there, go straight to the bar. The one on the left. Find Imperia."

I frowned. "Who's Imperia?"

"The succubus. Tell her you want to order a nightcap. She'll make sure you get home safely."

"A nightcap? What does that mean?"

"Just do it."

I exhaled slowly. "What will you do?"

His dark eyes held mine, and I felt his gaze all the way through my borrowed exterior and into my bones. The parts of me that were me—Gem—trembled at being so clearly seen even when I was wrapped inside someone or something else. Had anyone ever looked at me that way?

If they had, I hadn't looked like a 'roided out body-guard at the time.

I wasn't sure how that didn't matter now, but it didn't. This went beyond who I was on the outside. Somehow, he knew who I was on the inside. It was terrifying and amazing all at once.

My breath caught. "Listen, I—"

A hand closed over my ankle, yanking hard, and I barely swallowed the scream that rose up. My balance tilted, and the masked stranger's hands closed over my arms, steadying me before I could fall.

Wrenching my leg out of reach, I looked down to find Feldspar scrambling to his feet. The wound on his torso wasn't gone, but it was definitely closing up. He was moving like a man who hadn't been split open down the center.

"Shit," I said, realizing way too late the prevention spell must have included a self-heal clause.

Beside Feldspar, Kristoff's hellhound was already awake and snapping his canines at my masked friend.

I shifted back to my own form, using my newfound

agility and speed to charge forward, hands outstretched. I hit Feldspar just as he straightened to his full height, planting my palms on either side of the wound still stitching itself back together—and shoved as hard as I could.

Feldspar grunted. His arms flailed as he tried to regain his balance. I kept shoving, taking one step, then another toward the cliff's edge, driving him backward until there was nowhere left to go.

Feldspar's eyes widened.

At the last moment, his hand shot out and closed around Kristoff's back paw. The hellhound was yanked backward—just out of reach of the mystery man's fist. Kristoff let out a howl that drowned out Feldspar's groan.

I watched as both of them disappeared over the cliff's edge.

Even after their voices had gone silent, I stared into the mist. Numbness snaked through me, rendering me immobile. Even as my body returned to its former state, I couldn't seem to break free of the horrific replay going on in my mind. I'd never killed before, but my own lack of sensation or guilt over it scared me.

A hand closed around my wrist, pulling me back from the edge of the drop. I whirled, yanking my arm free before realizing it was only him. My new friend.

"It's over," he murmured. "You're okay."

I blew out a breath, shoving the mental images aside

for now. It was something I'd have to deal with later. "Thanks," I told him.

He nodded.

"That was..." I didn't know how to finish or where to begin for that matter.

Without offering a response, the man turned and began walking away.

"Wait!" I hurried after him. "Where are you going?"

He paused and cast a glance toward the sky. "It's almost time for the fireworks."

I cocked my head. "What happens after the fireworks?"

"All of this vanishes."

I blinked. "Just like that?"

His gaze settled on me again, his mouth set in a hard frown. The intensity from earlier was gone, replaced with obvious impatience. He wanted to be done with me—so why couldn't I just let him go? It was the smart play here, putting some distance between us. Give me a chance to get my bearings before I faced Rigo again.

"You never told me what you wanted," I said instead.

"For what?"

"For this," I said, waving my hand at the cliff. "For saving me. Nothing's free, so what do you want? Money? Sex? My firstborn?"

He let out a choking sound before catching himself

and inhaling sharply. "I don't want anything," he assured me.

"Good, because I'm not really planning on having kids at this point in my life. Money... Well, I think I could get you cab fare home. Long as you're not going too far. And the sex... I mean, I think it's safe to say I'm not in the mood considering I was almost literally pillaged tonight."

His mouth twitched slightly.

I narrowed my eyes, squinting to decipher whether he'd actually just smiled. But it was gone before I could be sure.

"You should get out of here before someone connects you to this," he said.

"What will you do now?"

"Go home," he said simply, but something told me that answer was anything but simple.

I wondered if Imperia was going to go with him. Maybe he'd get a nightcap from her like he'd suggested for me. At the thought, jealousy tightened my hands into fists.

Ridiculous, I realized. I had no clue who he was. To me, he was no one. And I was jealous of a date that may or may not be happening for him later.

"I don't even know your name," I blurted.

He stared at me, suspicion clouding the intensity of his gaze, dulling the sharp connection between us.

"I'm not going to tell anyone," I added. "I just want to know."

He continued to study me, and I stared back, fascinated at the range of emotions going on behind his stare. His expression never changed, but just like he had seen me earlier, I felt like I was seeing him—the real him. It terrified me in a way murder hadn't even been able to do.

My palms turned sweaty, and I resisted the urge to wipe them on my dress. I was positive that if I moved now, it would ruin this. So, I waited, barely breathing, while he seemed to work through whatever held him back.

Finally, he sighed. "It's—"

"Lita?" Footsteps behind me made me jump.

I whirled and then froze at the sight of Rigo striding toward me across the castle lawn.

"Rigo?"

His eyes went wide when he saw me, and I sucked in a sharp breath at what I must look like. I wasn't Feldspar's doppelgänger anymore, but I did still have his blood coating my legs—and probably other parts of me as well.

Not to mention the masked man beside me.

I snapped my head around to look at him, panicked at the idea of outing him to Rigo, but he was gone.

I stared at the curling fog where he'd stood a moment ago, my jaw half-open. I'd seen a lot in my short life. Heard about even more. Creatures who could turn into bats and fly away. Warlocks with the power to vanish in a puff of smoke. Shifters even more skilled than me who could turn into a tiny ant and crawl away without their enemy's notice. I'd never seen someone just evaporate into thin air before. But a quick scan around the foggy cliffside revealed nothing but empty air.

I had absolutely zero idea where he could have gone, supernatural creature or not, but I was out of time to figure it out.

Rigo grabbed my arm just above the elbow, yanking me back toward the castle. "Dammit, I've been looking everywhere for you," he hissed. "What the hell are you doing back here? And why aren't you answering comms?"

I let myself be pulled along, processing through all the explanations I could possibly give him about what had happened tonight.

"My comm's busted," I said.

"How in the hell did that happen?"

"Well, things didn't go exactly as planned," I said.

"You're damn skippy they didn't," he snapped. "What went on here?"

I opened my mouth, but he shut me down.

"No, you know what? Don't even try to answer me here. We're going back to base. You can give me a full debrief there. I don't want to take a chance on your mark seeing us together."

Not likely. But I decided against telling him that for now.

We hurried through the fog toward the castle, and I was surprised to see that a crowd had gathered on the back lawn. Most of the couples tucked away in the dark corners had come forward to join the others. A large portion of them had even removed their masks, and everyone stood around as if waiting for something to happen.

Rigo ignored them all and hurried me toward a side door standing open just ahead. I wondered if he'd noticed the blood on me yet or if it was too dark and foggy to tell.

Above us, a pop sounded in the sky. I looked up in time to see fireworks exploding in an array of glittery colors. The crowd gasped and then oohed and ahhed as the bursts of color continued to light up the sky. It really was beautiful.

My mind drifted back to the masked stranger. He'd known the fireworks were coming. Was he somewhere out there watching them now? Would I ever see him again? Part of me wanted to run back and look for him. Make him tell me his name.

I glanced down at Rodrigo still tugging me along. A deep frown had settled on his mouth, and I knew from the way he walked, head down, shoulders hunched, that he didn't give two shits about fireworks.

God, this debrief was going to suck.

TWENTY-THREE

The staging room was exactly as I'd left it right down to the tablet still lying on the edge of the counter. I glanced around at the space and then down at myself—no hiding the blood now. It was beginning to dry on my skin, and I had to resist the urge to scratch at it.

Rigo stood before me, also taking in the mess I'd made of myself.

I cleared my throat, hoping to divert his attention. "How did we get back?"

A few seconds ago, we'd passed through the side door that led into the castle—and we'd ended up here. I wasn't sure how Rigo had managed a portal without the proper permits. Then again, stranger things had happened. Tonight, especially.

Rodrigo stood with his hands on his hips. "We're safe, and that's all that matters. Now, did you get the package?"

No mention of the blood on my legs.

"I did."

"Well?" he prompted.

I sighed and dug the computer chip out of my dress, ignoring the awkwardness of having Rigo watch me do it. I handed it over and glared at his raised brows and quirked lips.

"Don't even think about making a comment right now," I muttered.

He took the chip and wisely kept his mouth shut. I watched as he peered at the tiny black square I'd given him, holding it up to the light as if that would yield its secrets.

"Good work," he said before pocketing the thing.

A small sliver of triumph surged inside me, but I tucked it away and braced myself for the rest of his questions.

Rigo reached for the tablet on the counter and swiped the screen. It lit up and displayed a menu. I waited while he tapped a few buttons that pulled up a voice recorder app. He hit the record button and then set it aside, looking up at me.

"Now, walk me through what happened," he said. "Don't leave anything out."

I left plenty out—mostly anything involving Jax McGuire or the masked stranger—but I did tell him about Kristoff and Feldspar dragging me into the soundproofed hallway to rough me up. And about the mystery liquid Kristoff had drugged me with.

I was still pissed about that.

"How in the hell did he know you were an agent?" Rodrigo demanded when I told him about Kristoff grabbing my comm unit from inside my ear.

"I was going to ask you the same thing," I countered.

Rodrigo shook his head, muttering a string of curses and threats against whoever had sold me out. "So he knew what you were after, and he knew the SSF were the ones who wanted it? Dammit. We need to brief a team on damage control."

"Actually," I licked my lips, and then forced myself to say, "I don't think it'll be a problem for us. He's not going to leak it or anything."

"Of course he's going to leak it. Probably to someone who has it out for SSF. Not to mention the fact that we used an untested agent for the op—"

"Trust me, Rigo. The op is safe."

His eyes narrowed as my words struck home. "What do you mean?"

I bit my lip and then made a face when I tasted blood. Angel above, I must look like a hot mess. "Look," I began. "Before I tell you, I want to remind you that my mission was to retrieve the data chip and deliver it to you. I did that. So, I've officially passed my test."

"Keep talking," he ordered.

I sighed. "The mark has been eliminated."

Rodrigo's eyes widened, and his mouth opened a full three seconds before any sound came out. "Are you fucking kidding me? You were instructed, no, *ordered*, to keep him alive!"

"It was him or me, Rigo. He knew who I was, and he wasn't—"

"He couldn't have actually harmed you. Not with the magic in that castle spelled against it."

"That magic doesn't have anything against wounds, even fatal wounds," I shot back. "Or did you not notice that I'm covered in blood?"

"We were getting to that," he said.

I resisted the urge to roll my eyes. "Kristoff's hound wasn't going to let this go. You know how a hellhound works once he's scented his own bloodlust. If he hadn't finished me tonight, he would have just been waiting in my apartment when I got home. He knew me, Rigo. My real name. What the hell was I supposed to do? Just wait for him to come back and finish the job?"

Rigo didn't answer, but his glare spoke volumes about his opinion. "How in the hell did you manage to actually kill him?" he asked finally.

Shit. This was the delicate part. "The magic only extends to the edge of the grounds," I said lightly.

Rigo's eyes bored into mine.

I forced my hands to my sides, standing at attention

when all I wanted to do was stomp my foot. Finally, I said, "He went over the cliffside, okay?"

"You mean, you pushed him over." His voice was deadly quiet.

I nodded, my eyes locked on a spot on the floor rather than on him.

"And his second? Feldspar?" he prompted.

My head snapped up. "You knew he'd brought his guard, and you didn't warn me?"

"I can't hold your hand in the field," he snapped. "Much as you might like me to."

I shook my head, trying to ignore the revulsion. Even now, he wasn't above innuendos. Asshole. "Both of them went over the cliff. It was me or them, and I made a choice." My chin came up, and I added, "I don't regret it either."

Rodrigo ran his tongue over his front teeth—something he only did when he was too pissed to actually say words.

Dammit.

Temper leaked out of me because the bottom line was that I'd screwed up. I'd been ordered not to harm the mark, and I'd done a lot more than harm him. Now, all I could do was stand here in silence and hope I hadn't totally fucked myself out of graduating.

The silence between us stretched.

Finally, he reached out and hit the button on the tablet to end the recording. I had a feeling that wasn't a good sign considering we weren't officially done with our debrief.

I waited, but Rigo didn't say a word to me. Instead, he slid his cell out of his pocket and made a quick call. I listened, impatient and a little sick, trying to decipher what was happening based on his end of things.

"Carter?" Rigo barked into his phone. "Yeah, I need a cleanup crew in the ravine behind the party site." He paused, flicking an angry glare at me before saying, "Actually, this one's a double."

Then he turned his back and began pacing as he said, "One more thing. You have any openings over there?"

My stomach tightened.

Rodrigo listened to the response on the other end and then said, "Uh-huh, I see. Fine. I don't give a shit about that. Make it happen." A pause and then, "We'll talk Monday."

He ended the call and spun to face me. A slow smile spread over his face. I had no idea how, but it managed to exist there even through the cold fury that remained underneath. "Congrats, Hawkins. You've officially graduated."

I blinked, trying to decipher what the hell had just happened. "Then why does it feel like I'm getting expelled?"

"Why would you be expelled? You said it yourself, you passed the mission."

His words were way too casual. My heart rate sped. My palms went clammy. This was way too easy—which meant this was bad.

"Rigo, what's going on? Who was that on the phone, and why did you ask if they had an opening?"

His smile widened, revealing way too much teeth to be genuine. "Now that you're an agent, you've been assigned an official post."

"And what post is that?" I asked even though I was fairly certain I didn't want to know.

"Cleaner. You report first thing Monday."

"What the hell is a cleaner?" I asked.

But the words were bitter on my tongue. Whatever it was—it wasn't a detective. And that was all that mattered.

"Exactly what it sounds like." Rigo's eyes narrowed. "The mess you made out on that cliff tonight? It'll have to be cleaned up before any humans can stumble upon it. And that doesn't just happen by magic." He snickered at his own bad joke. "You know what it does take?"

In the short pause that followed, I didn't answer, but he didn't want me to. He was enjoying this way too much to let me get a word in now. "It takes hard work. Grunt work. And that work falls to someone in the SSF. Starting Monday, that someone will be you."

My heart sank straight into my knees. Everything I'd worked for had been for this. Becoming an agent. No, not just an agent. Detective.

I had to get to headquarters. And this cleaner position sounded a long way off from that. Too long. In fact, considering the fact that I'd never even heard of the job, I had a feeling cleaners weren't exactly moving up the corporate ladder.

"You can't do this," I said.

"I can, and I did," Rodrigo snapped, his smile vanishing.

In its place was grim satisfaction, and I had to swallow the surprise in seeing it so blatantly displayed. He'd despised me all this time, and now he wasn't doing anything to hide it. At least before, there'd been a semblance of professionalism—well, when he wasn't hitting on me anyway—but now there was only disgust and dismissal.

"I completed the mission," I argued. "I deserve to be promoted to detective—"

"You deserve to be expelled. Or maybe even memory-wiped." I twitched at that, my jaw going slack, but he went on before I could respond. "You were ordered to keep your hands off Rasmussen, and you disregarded that order. No detective would get away with that, which means you're clearly not top agent material. You are, however, great at making messes." The smile ghosted its way back to his lips. "It only makes sense you learn to clean them up."

I fought the urge to scream. This was not happening.

"This is bullshit," I said quietly. "It's revenge, plain and simple. You don't give two shits about Rasmussen."

Rigo's answering glare said it all.

His response was slow and calculated. "You know, there is a way you could reinstate your status. Maybe even promote yourself here and now, and we can forget this whole cleaner business was even discussed."

If he suggested a date or anything remotely similar, I was going to deck him. "What?" I snapped.

"Tell me who helped you."

I blinked, caught off guard.

"You couldn't have known about the magic's loophole without help," Rodrigo added. "Tell me who told you, and I'll consider promoting you to permits."

"Permits?"

That job was paperwork, pure and simple. Maybe he considered it a step up from cleaner, but glorified secretary wasn't good enough.

He took a step closer. "Who told you about the loophole, Gem?"

I thought about the masked stranger. About those eyes that had seen right through my artificial exterior. Unlike Rigo and so many others, he hadn't cared at all about my physical appearance. He'd looked right past it and saw the real me.

"No one helped me," I said firmly.

Rigo frowned. "Look, if you're protecting someone, I get it, but you should think of your own—"

"I'm not protecting anyone," I insisted. "Is it so hard to believe I could figure out something like that for myself? You did train me to think outside the box."

He cleared his throat and picked up the tablet, heading for the stairs. "So be it. You'll pack your things and report to your new post first thing Monday. Oh and leave the dress and your comm unit with Starla. Nothing here is yours to keep."

I bit back a nasty response, hating that it had come to this—with my fate in the hands of someone like Rodrigo Garcia.

Someday...

I promised myself that one word just like I'd done for the past three months of training. Only now, someday sounded a lot farther off.

A cleaner.

I had no idea what the job entailed, but I was positive I wasn't going to like it.

At the top of the stairs, Rigo turned back, looking down on me with that same disgusted satisfaction. "If it makes you feel any better, you were one of the most entertaining recruits I've ever had," he said. "Tonight was a shitshow, but at least no one can ever say you're predictable."

I scowled. "You know, I thought they said what happens at The Monster Ball stays at The Monster Ball."

His smile was so smug, I had to clasp my hands together to keep from rushing up the stairs and smashing them into his face. "For you," he said, "It's more like what happens at The Monster Ball haunts you for life. Good night, Gem. I'll see you at the annual Christmas party. Hopefully, you'll have cleaned up by then."

The last thing I heard was his laughter echoing off the walls of the elevator shaft as he stepped inside. And I knew I hadn't earned the future I'd wanted so badly. All I'd done was trade one prison for another. *Someday*, I vowed, I'd find my father's killer, and then I'd break free. And when I did, Rodrigo would be the first casualty of my escape.

The End
Look for the next book, Knock 'Em Dead!

ABOUT THE AUTHOR

Heather Hildenbrand was born and raised in a small town in northern Virginia where she was homeschooled through high school. (She's only slightly socially awkward as a result.) She writes paranormal and contemporary romance with plenty of abs and angst. Her most frequent hobbies are riding motorcycles and avoiding killer slugs.

You can find out more about Heather and her books at heatherhildenbrand.com.

the other wants to kill him. Can siblings survive rivalry and forbidden love?

A Risk Worth Taking: A New Adult Contemporary Romance with southern charm and a hippie farmer capable of swoon and heartbreak in the same breath.

Dirty Blood: A Young Adult Paranormal Romance about a girl who falls in love with a werewolf, only to find out she's a Hunter, born and bred to kill the very thing she means to save.

Imitation: A Young Adult SciFi Romance with life or death choices and a conspiracy so deep, even a motorcycle-riding bodyguard can't pull you out.

O Face: Is Summerville's most eligible bachelor hot enough to melt the ice princess herself?

For a complete list of titles, visit www.heatherhildenbrand.com.